Edward

Crusoe in New York and Other Tales

Edward Everett Hale

Crusoe in New York and Other Tales

1st Edition | ISBN: 978-3-75234-541-4

Place of Publication: Frankfurt am Main, Germany

Year of Publication: 2020

Outlook Verlag GmbH, Germany.

CRUSOE IN NEW YORK,

AND OTHER TALES.

BY

EDWARD E. HALE

PREFACE.

So far as these little stories have met the public eye, they have called forth criticism from two points of view. It is said, on the one hand, that the moral protrudes too obviously; that if a preacher wants to preach, he had better preach and be done with it; that, in the nineteenth century, which is given to realism, nobody wants "invented example," or stories written to enforce certain theories of right. It is said, on the other hand, that the stories have no right to be, because they have no purpose; that nobody can tell what the author is driving at,—perhaps he cannot tell himself; and that, in the nineteenth century, nobody has any right to thrust upon an exhausted world stories which are not true unless they teach a lesson.

It was early settled for me by the critics, in my little experience as a story-writer, that it is wrong for an author to make his stories probable,—that he who does this is "a forger and a counterfeiter." There is, however, high authority for teaching by parable—and that parable which has a very great air of probability.

My limited experience as an editor has taught me, that, whatever else people will read or will not read, they do read short stories, on the whole, more than they read anything else,—nineteenth century to the contrary notwithstanding.

Whether these little tales have any right to be or not, they exist. To those who think they should have been cast in the shape of sermons, I have only to say that there also exist already, in that form of instructions, one thousand and ninety-six short essays by the same author, to which number every week of his strength and health makes an addition. These are open to the perusal or the hearing of any person who is not "partial to stories," to use an expressive national dialect. Some few even are for sale in print by the publishers of these tales.

The little book is dedicated, with the author's thanks, to those kind readers who have followed his earlier stories, and have been so tolerant that they were willing to ask for more.

MATUNUCK ON THE HILL, RHODE ISLAND,
    July 15, 1880.

PART I.

I was born in the year 1842, in the city of New York, of a good family, though not of that country, my father being a foreigner of Bremen, who settled first in England. He got a good estate by merchandise, and afterward lived at New York. But first he had married my mother, whose relations were named Robinson—a very good family in her country—and from them I was named.

My father died before I can remember—at least, I believe so. For, although I sometimes figure to myself a grave, elderly man, thickset and wearing a broad-brimmed hat, holding me between his knees and advising me seriously, I cannot say really whether this were my father or no; or, rather, whether this is really some one I remember or no. For my mother, with whom I have lived alone much of my life, as the reader will see, has talked to me of my father so much, and has described him to me so faithfully, that I cannot tell but it is her description of him that I recollect so easily. And so, as I say, I cannot tell whether I remember him or no.

He never lost his German notions, and perhaps they gained in England some new force as to the way in which boys should be bred. At least, for myself, I know that he left to my mother strict charge that I should be bound 'prentice to a carpenter as soon as I was turned of fourteen. I have often heard her say that this was the last thing he spoke to her of when he was dying; and, with the tears in her eyes, she promised him it should be so. And though it cost her a world of trouble—so changed were times and customs—to find an old-fashioned master who would take me for an apprentice, she was as good as her word.

I should like to tell the story of my apprenticeship, if I supposed the reader cared as much about it as I do; but I must rather come to that part of my life which is remarkable, than hold to that which is more like the life of many other boys. My father's property was lost or was wasted, I know not how, so that my poor mother had but a hard time of it; and when I was just turned of twenty-one and was free of my apprenticeship, she had but little to live upon but what I could bring home, and what she could earn by her needle. This was no grief to me, for I was fond of my trade, and I had learned it well. My old master was fond of me, and would trust me with work of a good deal of responsibility. I neither drank nor smoked, nor was I overfond of the amusements which took up a good deal of the time of my fellow-workmen. I was most pleased when, on pay-day, I could carry home to my mother ten, fifteen, or even twenty dollars—could throw it into her lap, and kiss her and make her kiss me.

"Here is the oil for the lamp, my darling," I would say; or, "Here is the grease for the wheels"; or, "Now you must give me white sugar twice a day." She was a good manager, and she made both ends meet very well.

I had no thought of leaving my master when my apprenticeship was over, nor had he any thought of letting me go. We understood each other well, he liked me and I liked him. He knew that he had in me one man who was not afraid of work, as he would say, and who would not shirk it. And so, indeed, he would often put me in charge of parties of workmen who were much older than I was.

So it was that it happened, perhaps some months after I had become a journeyman, that he told me to take a gang of men, whom he named, and to go quite up-town in the city, to put a close wooden fence around a vacant lot of land there. One of his regular employers had come to him, to say that this lot of land was to be enclosed, and the work was to be done by him. He had sent round the lumber, and he told me that I would find it on the ground. He gave me, in writing, the general directions by which the fence was ordered, and told me to use my best judgment in carrying them out. "Only take care," said he, "that you do it as well as if I was there myself. Do not be in a hurry, and be sure your work stands."

I was well pleased to be left thus to my own judgment. I had no fear of failing to do the job well, or of displeasing my old master or his employer. If I had any doubts, they were about the men who were to work under my lead, whom I did not rate at all equally; and, if I could have had my pick, I should have thrown out some of the more sulky and lazy of them, and should have chosen from the other hands. But youngsters must not be choosers when they are on their first commissions.

I had my party well at work, with some laborers whom we had hired to dig our post-holes, when a white-haired old man, with gold spectacles and a broad-brimmed hat, alighted from a cab upon the sidewalk, watched the men for a minute at their work, and then accosted me. I knew him perfectly, though of course he did not remember me. He was, in fact, my employer in this very job, for he was old Mark Henry, a Quaker gentleman of Philadelphia, who was guardian of the infant heirs who owned this block of land which we were enclosing. My master did all the carpenter's work in the New York houses which Mark Henry or any of his wards owned, and I had often seen him at the shop in consultation. I turned to him and explained to him the plans for the work. We had already some of the joists cut, which were to make the posts to our fence. The old man measured them with his cane, and said he thought they would not be long enough.

I explained to him that the fence was to be eight feet high, and that these were quite long enough for that.

"I know," he said, "I know, my young friend, that my order was for a fence eight feet high, but I do not think that will do."

With some surprise I showed him, by a "ten-foot pole," how high the fence would come.

"Yes, my young friend, I see, I see. But I tell thee, every beggar's brat in the ward will be over thy fence before it has been built a week, and there will be I know not what devices of Satan carried on in the inside. All the junk from the North River will be hidden there, and I shall be in luck if some stolen trunk, nay, some dead man's body, is not stowed away there. Ah, my young friend, if thee is ever unhappy enough to own a vacant lot in the city, thee will know much that thee does not know now of the exceeding sinfulness of sin. Thee will know of trials of the spirit and of the temper that thee has never yet experienced."

I said I thought this was probable, but I thought inwardly that I would gladly be tried that way. The old man went on:—

"I said eight feet to friend Silas, but thee may say to him that I have thought better of it, and that I have ordered thee to make the fence ten feet high. Thee may say that I am now going to Philadelphia, but that I will write to him my order when I arrive. Meanwhile thee will go on with the fence as I bid thee."

And so the old man entered his cab again, and rode away.

I amused myself at his notion, for I knew very well that the street-boys and other loafers would storm his ten-foot wall as readily as they would have stormed the Malakoff or the Redan, had they supposed there was anything to gain by doing it. I had, of course, to condemn some of my posts, which were already cut, or to work them in to other parts of the fence. My order for spruce boards was to be enlarged by twenty per cent by the old man's direction, and this, as it happened, led to a new arrangement of my piles of lumber on my vacant land.

And all this it was which set me to thinking that night, as I looked on the work, that I might attempt another enterprise, which, as it proved, lasted me for years, and which I am now going to describe.

I had worked diligently with the men to set up some fifty feet of the fence where it parted us from an alley-way, for I wanted a chance to dry some of the boards, which had just been hauled from a raft in the North River. The truckmen had delivered them helter-skelter, and they lay, still soaking, above each other on our vacant lot.

We turned all our force on this first piece of fence, and had so much of it done that, by calling off the men just before sundown, I was able to set up all the wet boards, each with one end resting on the fence and the other on the ground, so that they took the air on both sides, and would dry more quickly. Of course this left a long, dark tunnel underneath.

As the other hands gathered up their tools and made ready to go, a fellow named McLoughlin, who had gone out with one of the three months' regiments not long before, said:—

"I would not be sorry to sleep there. I have slept in many a worse place than that in Dixie"; and on that he went away, leaving me to make some measurements which I needed the next day. But what he said rested in my mind, and, as it happened, directed the next twelve years of my life.

Why should not I live here? How often my mother had said that, if she had only a house of her own, she should be perfectly happy! Why should not we have a house of our own here, just as comfortable as if we had gone a thousand miles out on the prairie to build it, and a great deal nearer to the book-stores, to the good music, to her old friends, and to my good wages? We had talked a thousand times of moving together to Kansas, where I was to build a little hut for her, and we were to be very happy together. But why not do as the minister had bidden us only the last Sunday—seize on to-day, and take what Providence offered now?

I must acknowledge that the thought of paying any ground rent to old Mr. Henry did not occur to me then—no, nor for years afterward. On the other hand, all that I thought of was this,—that here was as good a chance as there was in Kansas to live without rent, and that rent had been, was still, and was likely to be my bugbear, unless I hit on some such scheme as this for abating it.

The plan, to be short, filled my mind. There was nothing in the way of house-building which I shrank from now, for, in learning my trade, I had won my Aladdin's lamp, and I could build my mother a palace, if she had needed one. Pleased with my fancy, before it was dark I had explored my principality from every corner, and learned all its capabilities.

The lot was an oblong, nearly three times as long as it was wide. On the west side, which was one of the short sides, it faced what I will call the Ninety-ninth Avenue, and on the south side, what I will call Fernando Street, though really it was one of the cross-streets with numbers. Running to the east it came to a narrow passage-way which had been reserved for the accommodation of the rear of a church which fronted on the street just north of us. Our back line was also the back line of the yards of the houses on the same street, but on our northeast corner the church ran back as far as the back line of both houses and yards, and its high brick wall—nearly fifty feet high —took the place there of the ten-foot brick wall, surmounted by bottle-glass, which made their rear defence.

The moment my mind was turned to the matter, I saw that in the rear of the church there was a corner, which lay warmly and pleasantly to the southern and western sun, which was still out of eye-shot from the street, pleasantly removed from the avenue passing, and only liable to inspection, indeed, from the dwelling-houses on the opposite side of our street,—houses which, at this moment, were not quite finished, though they would be occupied soon.

If, therefore, I could hit on some way of screening my mother's castle from them—for a castle I called it from the first moment, though it was to be much more like a cottage—I need fear no observation from other quarters; for the avenue was broad, and on the other side from us there was a range of low, rambling buildings—an engine-house and a long liquor-saloon were two—which had but one story. Most of them had been built, I suppose, only to earn something for the land while it was growing valuable. The church had no windows in the rear, and that protected my castle—which was, indeed, still in the air—from all observation on that side.

I told my mother nothing of all this when I went home. But I did tell her that I had some calculations to make for my work, and that was enough. She went on, sweet soul! without speaking a word, with her knitting and her sewing, at her end of the table, only getting up to throw a cloth over her parrot's cage when he was noisy; and I sat at my end of the table, at work over my figures, as silent as if I had been on a desert island.

Before bedtime I had quite satisfied myself with the plan of a very pretty little house which would come quite within our space, our means, and our shelter. There was a little passage which ran quite across from east to west. On the church side of this there was my mother's kitchen, which was to be what I fondly marked the "common-room." This was quite long from east to west, and not more than half as long the other way. But on the east side, where I could have no windows, I cut off, on its whole width, a deep closet; and this proved a very fortunate thing afterward, as you shall see. On the west side I made one large square window, and there was, of course, a door into the passage.

On the south side of the passage I made three rooms, each narrow and long. The two outside rooms I meant to light from the top. Whether I would put any skylight into the room between them, I was not quite so certain; I did not expect visitors in my new house, so I did not mark it a "guest-room" in the plan. But I thought of it as a storeroom, and as such, indeed, for many years we used it; though at last I found it more convenient to cut a sky-light in the roof there also. But I am getting before my story.

Before I had gone to bed that night I had made a careful estimate as to how much lumber I should need, of different kinds, for my little house; for I had, of course, no right to use my master's lumber nor Mr. Henry's; nor had I any thought of doing so. I made out an estimate that would be quite full, for shingles, for clapboards, white pine for my floors and finish,—for I meant to make good a job of it if I made any,—and for laths for the inside work. I made another list of the locks, hinges, window furniture and other hardware I should need; but for this I cared less, as I need not order them so soon. I could scarcely refrain from showing my plan to my mother, so snug and comfortable did it look already; but I had already determined that the "city house" should be a present to her on her next birthday, and that till then I would keep it a secret from her, as from all the world; so I refrained.

The next morning I told my master what the old Quaker had directed about the fence, and I took his order for the new lumber we should need to raise the height as was proposed. At the same time I told him that we were all annoyed at the need of carrying our tools back and forth, and because we could only take the nails for one day's use; and that, if he were willing, I had a mind to risk an old chest I had with the nails in it and a few tools, which I thought I could so hide that the wharf-rats and other loafers should not discover it. He told me to do as I pleased, that he would risk the nails if I would risk my tools; and so, by borrowing what we call a hand-cart for a few days, I was able to take up my own little things to the lot without his asking any other questions, or without exciting the curiosity of McLoughlin or any other of the men. Of course, he would have sent up in the shop-wagon anything we needed; but it was far out of the way, and nobody wanted to drive the team back at night if we could do without. And so, as night came on, I left the men at their work, and having loaded my hand-cart with a small chest I had, I took that into the alley-way of which I told you before, carried my box of tools into the corner between the church and our fence, under the boards which we had set up to-day, and covered it heavily, with McLoughlin's help, with joists and boards, so that no light work would remove them, if, indeed, any wanderer of the night suspected that the box was there. I took the hand-cart out into the alley-way and chained it, first by the wheel and then by the handle, in two staples which I drove there. I had another purpose in this, as you shall see; but most of all, I wanted to test both the police and the knavishness of the neighborhood, by seeing if the hand-cart were there in the morning.

To my great joy it was, and to my greater joy it remained there unmolested all the rest of the week in which we worked there. For my master, who never came near us himself, increased our force for us on the third day, so that at the end of the week, or Saturday night, the job was nearly done, and well done, too.

On the third day I had taken the precaution to throw out in the inside of our inclosure a sort of open fence, on which I could put the wet boards to dry, which at first I had placed on our side fence. I told McLoughlin, what was true enough, that the south sun was better for them than the sun from the west. So I ran out what I may call a screen thirty-five feet from the church, and parallel with it, on which I set up these boards to dry, and to my great joy I saw that they would wholly protect the roof of my little house from any observation from the houses the other side of the way while the workmen were at work, or even after they were inhabited.

There was not one of the workmen with me who had forethought enough or care for our master's interest to ask whose boards those were which we left there, or why we left them there. Indeed, they knew the next Monday that I went up with Fergus, the Swede, to bring back such lumber as we did not use, and none of them knew or cared how much we left there.

For me, I was only eager to get to work, and that day seemed very long to me. But that Monday afternoon I asked my master if I might have the team again for my own use for an hour or so, to move some stuff of mine and my mother's, and he gave it to me readily.

I had then only to drive up-town to a friendly lumberman's, where my own stuff was already lying waiting for me to load up, with the assistance of the workmen there, and to drive as quickly as I could into the church alley. Here I looked around, and seeing a German who looked as if he were only a day from Bremen, I made signs to him that if he would help me I would give him a piece of scrip which I showed him. The man had been long enough in the country to know that the scrip was good for lager. He took hold manfully with me, and carried my timbers and boards into the inclosure through a gap I made in the fence for the purpose. I gave him his money, and he went away. As he went to Minnesota the next day, he never mentioned to anybody the business he had been engaged in.

Meanwhile, I had bought my hand-cart of the man who owned it. I left a little pile of heavy cedar logs on the outside, spiking them to each other, indeed, that they should not be easily moved. And to them and to my posts I padlocked the hand-cart; nor was it ever disturbed during my reign in those regions. So I had easy method enough when I wanted a bundle or two of laths, or a bunch of shingles, or anything else for my castle, to bring them up in the cool of the evening, and to discharge my load without special observation. My pile of logs, indeed, grew eventually into a blind or screen, which quite protected that corner of the church alley from the view of any passer-by in Fernando Street.

Of that whole summer, happy and bright as it all was, I look back most often on the first morning when I got fairly to work on my new home. I told my mother that for some weeks I should have to start early, and that she must not think of getting up for my breakfast. I told her that there was extra work on a job up-town, and that I had promised to be there at five every day while the summer lasted. She left for me a pot of coffee, which I promised her I would warm when the time for breakfast and dinner came; and for the rest, she always had my dinner ready in my tin dinner-pail. Little did she know then, sweet saint! that I was often at Fernando Street by half-past three in the first sweet gray of those summer days.

On that particular day, it was really scarcely light enough for me to find the nail I drew from the plank which I left for my entrance. When I was fairly within and the plank was replaced, I felt that I was indeed monarch of all I surveyed. What did I survey? The church wall on the north; on the south, my own screen of spruce boards, now well dry; on the east and west, the ten-foot fence which I had built myself; and over there on the west, God's deep, transparent sky, in which I could still see a planet whose name I did not know. It was a heaven, indeed, which He had said was as much mine as his!

The first thing, of course, was to get out my frame. This was a work of weeks. The next thing was to raise it. And here the first step was the only hard one, nor was this so hard as it would seem. The highest wall of my house was no higher than the ten-foot fence we had already built on the church alley. The western wall, if, indeed, a frame house has any walls, was only eight feet high. For foundations and sills, I dug deep post-holes, in which I set substantial cedar posts which I knew would outlast my day, and I framed my sills into these. I made the frame of the western wall lie out upon the ground in one piece; and I only needed a purchase high enough, and a block with repeating pulleys strong enough, to be able to haul up the whole frame by my own strength, unassisted. The high purchase I got readily enough by making what we called a "three-leg," near twenty feet high, just where my castle was to stand. I had no difficulty in hauling this into its place by a solid staple and ring, which for this purpose I drove high in the church wall. My multiplying pulley did the rest; and after it was done, I took out the staple and mended the hole it had made, so the wall was as good as ever.

You see it was nobody's business what shanty or what tower old Mark Henry or the Fordyce heirs might or might not put on the vacant corner lot. The Fordyce heirs were all in nurseries and kindergartens in Geneva, and indeed would have known nothing of corner lots, had they been living in their palace in Fourteenth Street. As for Mark Henry, that one great achievement by which he rode up to Fernando Street was one of the rare victories of his life, of which ninety-nine hundredths were spent in counting-houses. Indeed, if he had gone there, all he would have seen was his ten-foot fence, and he would have taken pride to himself that he had it built so high.

When the day of the first raising came, and the frame slipped into the mortises so nicely, as I had foreordained that it should do, I was so happy that I could scarcely keep my secret from my mother. Indeed, that day I did run back to dinner. And when she asked me what pleased me so, I longed to let her know; but I only smoothed her cheeks with my hands, and kissed her on both of them, and told her it was because she was so handsome that I was so pleased. She said she knew I had a secret from her, and I owned that I had, but she said she would not try to guess, but would wait for the time for me to tell her.

And so the summer sped by. Of course I saw my sweetheart, as I then called my mother, less and less. For I worked till it was pitch-dark at the castle; and after it was closed in, so I could work inside, I often worked till ten o'clock by candlelight. I do not know how I lived with so little sleep; I am afraid I slept pretty late on Sundays. But the castle grew and grew, and the common-room, which I was most eager to finish wholly before cold weather, was in complete order three full weeks before my mother's birthday came.

Then came the joy of furnishing it. To this I had looked forward all the summer, and I had measured with my eye many a bit of furniture, and priced, in an unaffected way, many an impossible second-hand finery, so that I knew just what I could do and what I could not do.

My mother had always wanted a Banner stove. I knew this, and it was a great grief to me that she had none, though she would never say anything about it.

To my great joy, I found a second-hand Banner stove, No. 2, at a sort of old junk-shop, which was, in fact, an old curiosity shop, not three blocks away from Ninety-ninth Avenue. Some one had sold this to them while it was really as good as new, and yet the keeper offered it to me at half-price.

I hung round the place a good deal, and when the man found I really had money and meant something, he took me into all sorts of alleys and hiding-places, where he stored his old things away. I made fabulous bargains there, for either the old Jew liked me particularly, or I liked things that nobody else wanted. In the days when his principal customers were wharf-rats, and his principal business the traffic in old cordage and copper, he had hung out as a sign an old tavern-sign of a ship that had come to him. His place still went by the name of "The Ship," though it was really, as I say, a rambling, third-rate old furniture shop of the old-curiosity kind.

But after I had safely carried the Banner to my new house, and was sure the funnel drew well, and that the escape of smoke and sparks was carefully guarded, many a visit did I make to The Ship at early morning or late in the evening, to bring away one or another treasure which I had discovered there.

Under the pretence of new-varnishing some of my mother's most precious tables and her bureau, I got them away from her also. I knocked up, with my own hatchet and saw, a sitting-table which I meant to have permanent in the middle of the room, which was much more convenient than anything I could buy or carry.

And so, on the 12th of October, the eve of my mother's birthday, the common-room was all ready for her. In her own room I had a new carpet and a new set of painted chamber furniture, which I had bought at the maker's, and brought up piece by piece. It cost me nineteen dollars and a half, for which I paid him in cash, which indeed he wanted sadly.

So, on the morning of the 13th of October, I kissed my mother forty times, because that day she was forty years old. I told her that before midnight she should know what the great surprise was, and I asked her if she could hold out till then.

She let me poke as much fun at her as I chose, because she said she was so glad to have me at breakfast; and I stayed long after breakfast, for I had told my mother that it was her birthday, and that I should be late. And such a thing as my asking for an hour or two was so rare that I took it quite of course when I did ask. I came home early at night, too. Then I said,—

"Now, sweetheart, the surprise requires that you spend the night away from home with me. Perhaps, if you like the place, we will spend to-morrow there. So I will take Poll in her cage, and you must put up your night-things and take them in your hand."

She was surprised now, for such a thing as an outing over night had never been spoken of before by either of us.

"Why, Rob," she said, "you are taking too much pains for your old sweetheart, and spending too much money for her birthday. Now, don't you think that you should really have as good a time, say, if we went visiting together, and then came back here?"

For, you see, she never thought of herself at all; it was only what I should like most.

"No, sweetheart dear," said I. "It is not for me, this 13th of October, it is all for you. And to-night's outing is not for me, it is for you; and I think you will like it and I think Poll will like it, and I have leave for to-morrow, and we will stay away all to-morrow."

As for Tom-puss, I said, we would leave some milk where he could find it, and I would leave a bone or two for him. But I whistled Rip, my dog, after me. I took Poll's cage, my mother took her bag, and locked and left her door, unconscious that she was never to enter it again.

A Ninety-ninth Avenue car took us up to Fernando Street. It was just the close of twilight when we came there. I took my mother to Church Alley, muttered something about some friends, which she did not understand more than I did, and led her up the alley in her confused surprise. Then I pushed aside my movable board, and, while she was still surprised, led her in after me and slid it back again.

"What is it, dear Rob? Tell me—tell me!"

"This way, sweetheart, this way!" This was all I would say.

I drew her after me through the long passage, led her into the common-room, which was just lighted up by the late evening twilight coming in between the curtains of the great square window. Then I fairly pushed her to the great, roomy easy-chair which I had brought from The Ship, and placed it where she could look out on the evening glow, and I said,—

"Mother, dear, this is the surprise; this is your new home; and, mother dear, your own boy has made it with his own hands, all for you."

"But, Rob, I do not understand—I do not understand at all. I am so stupid. I know I am awake. But it is as sudden as a dream!"

So I had to begin and to explain it all,—how here was a vacant lot that Mark Henry had the care of, and how I had built this house for her upon it. And long before I had explained it all, it was quite dark. And I lighted up the pretty student's-lamp, and I made the fire in the new Banner with my own hands.

And that night I would not let her lift a kettle, nor so much as cut a loaf of bread. It was my feast, I said, and I had everything ready, round to a loaf of birthday-cake which I had ordered at Taylor's, which I had myself frosted and dressed, and decorated with the initials of my mother's name.

And when the feast was over, I had the best surprise of all. Unknown to my mother, I had begged from my Aunt Betsy my own father's portrait, and I had hung that opposite the window, and now I drew the curtain that hid it, and told my sweetheart that this and the house were her birthday presents for this year!

*　　　*　　　*　　　*　　　*

And this was the beginning of a happy life, which lasted nearly twelve years. I could make a long story of it, for there was an adventure in everything,—in the way we bought our milk, and the way we took in our coals. But there is no room for me to tell all that, and it might not interest other people as it does me. I am sure my mother was never sorry for the bold step she took when we moved there from our tenement. True, she saw little or no society, but she had not seen much before. The conditions of our life were such that she did not like to be seen coming out of Church Alley, lest people should ask how she got in, and excepting in the evening, I did not care to have her go. In the evening I could go with her. She did not make many calls, because she could not ask people to return them. But she would go with me to concerts, and to the church parlor meetings, and sometimes to exhibitions; and at such places, and on Sundays, she would meet, perhaps, one or another of the few friends she had in New York. But we cared for them less and less, I will own, and we cared more and more for each other.

As soon as the first spring came, I made an immense effort, and spaded over nearly half of the lot. It was ninety feet wide, and over two hundred and sixty long—more than half an acre. So I knew we could have our own fresh vegetables, even if we never went to market. My mother was a good gardener, and she was not afraid even to hoe the corn when I was out of the way. I dare say that the people whom the summer left in the street above us often saw her from their back windows, but they did not know—as how should they?—who had the charge of this lot, and there was no reason why they should be surprised to see a cornfield there. We only raised green corn. I am fond of Indian cake, but I did not care to grind my own corn, and I could buy sweet meal without trouble. I settled the milk question, after the first winter, by keeping our own goats. I fenced in, with a wire fence, the northwest corner of our little empire, and put there a milch goat and her two kids. The kids were pretty little things, and would come and feed from my mother's hand. We soon weaned them, so that we could milk their mother; and after that our flock grew and multiplied, and we were never again troubled for such little milk as we used.

Some old proprietor, in the old Dutch days, must have had an orchard in these parts. There were still left two venerable wrecks of ancient pear-trees; and although they bore little fruit, and what they bore was good for nothing, they still gave a compact and grateful shade. I sodded the ground around them, and made a seat beneath, where my mother would sit with her knitting all the afternoon. Indeed, after the sods grew firm, I planted hoops there, and many a good game of croquet have she and I had together there, playing so late that we longed for the chance they have in Sybaris, where, in the evening, they use balls of colored glass, with fire-flies shut up inside.

On the 11th of February, in the year 1867, my old master died, to my great regret, and I truly believe to that of his widow and her children. His death broke up the establishment, and I, who was always more of a cabinet-maker or joiner than carpenter or builder, opened a little shop of my own, where I took orders for cupboards, drawers, stairs, and other finishing work, and where I employed two or three German journeymen, and was thus much more master of my own time. In particular, I had two faithful fellows, natives of my own father's town of Bremen. While they were with me, I could leave them a whole afternoon at a time, while I took any little job there might be, and worked at it at my own house at home. Where my house was, except that it was far uptown, they never asked, nor ever, so far as I know, cared. This gave me the chance for many a pleasant afternoon with my mother, such as we had dreamed of in the old days when we talked of Kansas. I would work at the lathe or the bench, and she would read to me. Or we would put off the bench till the evening, and we would both go out into the cornfield together.

And so we lived year after year. I am afraid that we worshipped each other too much. We were in the heart of a crowded city, but there was that in our lives which tended a little to habits of loneliness, and I suppose a moralist would say that our dangers lay in that direction.

On the other hand, I am almost ashamed to say, that, as I sat in a seat I had made for myself in old Van der Tromp's pear-tree, I would look upon my corn and peas and squashes and tomatoes with a satisfaction which I believe many a nobleman in England does not enjoy.

Till the youngest of the Fordyce heirs was of age, and that would not be till 1880, this was all my own. I was, by right of possession and my own labors, lord of all this region. How else did the writers on political economy teach me that any property existed!

I surveyed it with a secret kind of pleasure. I had not abundance of pears; what I had were poor and few. But I had abundance of sweet corn, of tomatoes, of peas, and of beans. The tomatoes were as wholesome as they were plentiful, and as I sat I could see the long shelves of them which my mother had spread in the sun to ripen, that we might have enough of them canned when winter should close in upon us. I knew I should have potatoes enough of my own raising also to begin the winter with. I should have been glad of more. But as by any good day's work I could buy two barrels of potatoes, I did not fret myself that my stock was but small.

Meanwhile my stock in bank grew fast. Neither my mother nor I had much occasion to buy new clothes. We were at no charge for house-rent, insurance, or taxes. I remember that a Spanish gentleman, who was fond of me, for whom I had made a cabinet with secret drawers, paid me in moidores and pieces-of-eight, which in those times of paper were a sight to behold.

I carried home the little bag, and told my mother that this was a birthday present for her; indeed, that she was to put it all in her bed that night, that she might say she had rolled in gold and silver. She played with the pieces, and we used them to count with, as we played our game of cribbage.

"But really, Robin, boy," said she, "it is as the dirt under our feet. I would give it all for three or four pairs of shoes and stockings, such as we used to buy in York, but such as these Lynn-built shoes and steam-knit stockings have driven out of the market."

Indeed, we wanted very little in our desert home.

And so for many years we led a happy life, and we found more in life than would have been possible had we been all tangled up with the cords of artificial society. I say "we," for I am sure I did, and I think my dear mother did.

But it was in the seventh year of our residence in the hut that of a sudden I had a terrible shock or fright, and this I must now describe to you. It comes in about the middle of this history, and it may end this chapter.

It was one Sunday afternoon, when I had taken the fancy, as I often did of Sundays, to inspect my empire. Of course, in a certain way, I did this every time I climbed old Van der Tromp's pear-tree, and sat in my hawk's-nest there. But a tour of inspection was a different thing. I walked close round the path which I had made next the fence of the inclosure. I went in among my goats,—even entered the goat-house and played with my kids. I tried the boards of the fence and the timber-stays, to be sure they all were sound. I had paths enough between the rows of corn and potatoes to make a journey of three miles and half a furlong, with two rods more, if I went through the whole of them. So at half-past four on this fatal afternoon I bade my mother good-by, and kissed her. I told her I should not be back for two hours, because I was going to inspect my empire, and I set out happily.

But in less than an hour—I can see the face of the clock now: it was twenty-two minutes after five—I flung myself in my chair, panting for breath, and, as my mother said, as pale as if I had seen a ghost. But I told her it was worse than that.

I had come out from between two high rows of corn, which wholly covered me, upon a little patch which lay warm to the south and west, where I had some melons a-ripening, and was just lifting one of the melons, to be sure that the under surface did not rot, when close behind it I saw the print of a man's foot, which was very plain to be seen in the soft soil.

I stood like one thunderstruck, or as if I had seen an apparition. I listened; I looked round me. I could hear nothing but the roar of the omnibuses, nor could I see anything. I went up and down the path, but it was all one. I could see no other impression but that one. I went to it again, to see if there were any more, and to observe if it might not be my fancy. But there was no room for that, for there was exactly the print of an Englishman's hobnailed shoe,— the heavy heel, the prints of the heads of the nails. There was even a piece of patch which had been put on it, though it had never been half-soled.

How it came there I knew not; neither could I in the least imagine. But, as I say, like a man perfectly confused and out of myself, I rushed home into my hut, not feeling the ground I went upon. I fled into it like one pursued, and, as my mother said, when I fell into my chair, panting, I looked as if I had seen a ghost.

It was worse than that, as I said to her.

PART II.

I cannot well tell you how much dismay this sight of a footprint in the ground gave me, nor how many sleepless nights it cost me. All the time I was trying to make my mother think that there was no ground for anxiety, and yet all the time I was showing her that I was very anxious. The more I pretended that I was not troubled, the more absentminded, and so the more troubled, I appeared to her. And yet, if I made no pretence, and told her what I really feared, I should have driven her almost wild by the story of my terrors. To have our pretty home broken up, perhaps to be put in the newspapers—which was a lot that, so far, we had always escaped in our quiet and modest life—all this was more than she or I could bear to think of.

In the midst of these cogitations, apprehensions, and reflections, it came into my thoughts one day, as I was working at my shop down-town, with my men, that all this might be a chimera of my own, and that the foot might be the print of my own boot as I had left it in the soil some days before when I was looking at my melons. This cheered me up a little, too. I considered that I could by no means tell for certain where I had trod and where I had not, and that if at last this was the print of my own boot, I had played the part of those fools who strive to make stories of spectres, and then are themselves frightened at them more than anybody else.

So I returned home that day in very good spirits. I carried to my mother a copy of Frank Leslie's Illustrated Newspaper, which had in it some pictures that I knew would please her, and I talked with her, in as light-hearted a way as I could, to try to make her think that I had forgotten my alarm. And afterward we played two or three games of Egyptian solitaire at the table, and I went to bed unusually early. But, at the first break of day, when I fancied or hoped that she was still asleep, I rose quickly, and half-dressing myself, crept out to the melon-patch to examine again the imprint of the foot and to make sure that it was mine.

Alas! it was no more mine than it was Queen Victoria's. If it had only been cloven, I could easily have persuaded myself whose it was, so much grief and trouble had it cost me. When I came to measure the mark with my own boot, I found, just as I had seen before, that mine was not nearly so large as this mark was. Also, this was, as I have said, the mark of a heavy brogan—such as I never wore—and there was the mark of a strange patch near the toe, such as I had never seen, nor, indeed, have seen since, from that hour to this hour. All these things renewed my terrors. I went home like a whipped dog, wholly certain now that some one had found the secret of our home: we might be surprised in it before I was aware; and what course to take for my security I knew not.

As we breakfasted, I opened my whole heart to my mother. If she said so, I would carry all our little property, piece by piece, back to old Thunberg, the junk-dealer, and with her parrot and my umbrella we would go out to Kansas, as we used to propose. We would give up the game. Or, if she thought best, we would stand on the defensive. I would put bottle glass on the upper edges of the fences all the way round.

There were four or five odd revolvers at The Ship, and I would buy them all, with powder and buckshot enough for a long siege. I would teach her how to load, and while she loaded I would fire, till they had quite enough of attacking us in our home. Now it has all gone by, I should be ashamed to set down in writing the frightful contrivances I hatched for destroying these "creatures," as I called them, or, at least, frightening them, so as to prevent their coming thither any more.

"Robin, my boy," said my mother to me, when I gave her a chance at last, "if they came in here to-night—whoever 'they' may be—very little is the harm that they could do us. But if Mr. Kennedy and twenty of his police should come in here over the bodies of—five times five are twenty-five, twenty-five times eleven are—two hundred and seventy-five people whom you will have killed by that time, if I load as fast as thee tells me I can, why, Robin, my boy, it will go hard for thee and me when the day of the assizes comes. They will put handcuffs on thy poor old mother and on thee, and if they do not send thee to Jack Ketch, they will send thee to Bloomingdale."

I could not but see that there was sense in what she said. Anyway, it cooled me down for the time, and I kissed her and went to my work less eager, and, indeed, less anxious, than I had been the night before. As I went down-town in the car, I had a chance to ask myself what right I had to take away the lives of these poor savages of the neighborhood merely because they entered on my possessions. Was it their fault that they had not been apprenticed to carpenters? Could they help themselves in the arrangements which had left them savages? Had any one ever given them a chance to fence in an up-town lot? Was it, in a word, I said to myself—was it my merit or my good luck which made me as good as a landed proprietor, while the Fordyce heirs had their education? Such thoughts, before I came to my shop, had quite tamed me down, and when I arrived there I was quite off my design, and I concluded that I had taken a wrong measure in my resolution to attack the savages, as I had begun to call men who might be merely harmless loafers.

It was clearly not my business to meddle with them unless they first attacked me. This it was my business to prevent; if I were discovered and attacked, then I knew my duty.

With these thoughts I went into my shop that day, and with such thoughts as these, and with my mother's good sense in keeping me employed in pleasanter things than hunting for traces of savages, I got into a healthier way of thinking.

The crop of melons came in well, and many a good feast we had from them. Once and again I was able to carry a nice fresh melon to an old lady my mother was fond of, who now lay sick with a tertian ague.

Then we had the best sweet corn for dinner every day that any man had in New York. For, at Delmonico's itself, the corn the grandees had had been picked the night before, and had started at two o'clock in the morning on its long journey to town. But my mother picked my corn just at the minute when she knew I was leaving my shop. She husked it, and put it in the pot, and, by the time I had come home, had slipped up the board in the fence that served me for a door, and had washed my face and hands in my own room, she would have dished her dinner, would have put her fresh corn upon the table, covered with a pretty napkin; and so, as I say, I had a feast which no nabob in New York had. No, indeed, nor any king that I know of, unless it were the King of the Sandwich Islands, and I doubt if he were as well served as I.

So I became more calm and less careworn, though I will not say but sometimes I did look carefully to see if I could find the traces of a man's foot; but I never saw another.

Unless we went out somewhere during the evening we went to bed early. We rose early as well, for I never lost the habits of my apprenticeship. And so it happened that we were both sound asleep in bed one night, when a strange thing happened, and a sudden fright came to us, of which I must tell quite at length, for it made, indeed, a very sudden change in the current of our lives.

I was sound asleep, as I said, and so, I found, was my mother also. But I must have been partly waked by some sudden noise in the street, for I knew I was sitting up in my bed, in the darkness, when I heard a woman scream,—a terrible cry,—and while I was yet startled, I heard her scream again, as if she were in deadly fear. My window was shaded by a heavy green curtain, but in an instant I had pulled it up, and, by the light of the moon, I seized my trousers and put them on.

I was well awake by this time, and when I flung open the door of my house, so as to run into my garden, I could hear many wild voices, some in English, some in German, some in Irish, and some with terrible cries, which I will not pretend I could understand.

There was no cry of a woman now, but only the howling of angry or drunken men, when they are in a rage with some one or with each other. What startled me was that, whereas the woman's cry came from the street south of me, which I have called Fernando Street, the whole crowd of men, as they howled and swore, were passing along that street rapidly, and then stopped for an instant, as if they were coming up what I called Church Alley. There must have been seven or eight of them.

Now, it was by Church Alley that my mother and I always came into our house, and so into our garden. In the eight years, or nearly so, that I had lived there, I had by degrees accumulated more and more rubbish near the furthest end of the alley as a screen, so to speak, that when my mother or I came in or out, no one in the street might notice us. I had even made a little wing-fence, out from my own, to which my hand-cart was chained. Next this I had piled broken brickbats and paving-stones, and other heavy things, that would not be stolen. There was the stump and the root of an old pear-tree there, too heavy to steal, and too crooked and hard to clean or saw. There was a bit of curbstone from the street, and other such trash, which quite masked the fence and the hand-cart.

On the other side—that is, the church side, or the side furthest from the street —was the sliding-board in the fence, where my mother and I came in. So soon as it was slid back, no man could see that the fence was not solid.

At this moment in the night, however, when I found that this riotous, drunken crew were pausing at the entrance of Church Alley, as doubting if they would not come down, I ran back through the passage knocking loudly for my mother as I passed, and, coming to my coal-bin, put my eye at the little hole through which I always reconnoitred before I slid the door. I could see nothing, nor at night ought I to have expected to do so.

But I could hear, and I heard what I did not expect. I could hear the heavy panting of one who had been running, and as I listened I heard a gentle low voice sob out, "Ach, ach, mein Gott! Ach, mein Gott!" or words that I thought were these, and I was conscious, when I tried to move the door, that some one was resting close upon it.

All the same, I put my shoulder stoutly to the cross-bar, to which the boards of the door were nailed; I slid it quickly in its grooves, and as it slid, a woman fell into the passage.

She was wholly surprised by the motion, so that she could not but fall. I seized her and dragged her in, saying, "Hush, hush, hush!" as I did so. But not so quick was I but that she screamed once more as I drew to the sliding-door

21

and thrust in the heavy bolt which held it.

In an instant my mother was in the passage, with a light in her hand. In another instant I had seized the light and put it out. But that instant was enough for her and me to see that here was a lovely girl, with no hat or bonnet on, with her hair floating wildly, both her arms bleeding, and her clothes all stained with blood. She could see my mother's face of amazement, and she could see my finger on my mouth, as with the other I dashed out the candle. We all thought quickly, and we all knew that we must keep still.

But that unfortunate scream of hers was enough. Though no one of us all uttered another sound, this was like a "view-halloo," to bring all those dogs down upon us. The passage was dark, and, to my delight, I heard some of them breaking their shins over the curbstone and old pear-tree of my defences. But they were not such hounds as were easily thrown off the scent, and there were enough to persevere while the leaders picked themselves up again.

Then how they swore and cursed and asked questions! And we three stood as still as so many frightened rabbits. In an instant more, one of them, who spoke in English, said he would be hanged if he thought she had gone into the church, that he believed she had got through the fence; and then, with his fist, or something harder, he began trying the boards on our side, and others of them we could hear striking those on the other side of the alley-way.

When it came to this, I whispered to my mother that she must never fear, only keep perfectly still. She dragged the frightened girl into our kitchen, which was our sitting-room, and they both fell, I know not how, into the great easy-chair.

For my part, I seized the light ladder, which always hung ready at the door, and ran with it at my full speed to the corner of Fernando Street and the alley. I planted the ladder, and was on the top of the fence in an instant.

Then I sprang my watchman's rattle, which had hung by the ladder, and I whirled it round well. It wholly silenced the sound of the swearing fellows up the passage, and their pounding. When I found they were still, I cried out:—

"This way, 24! this way, 47! I have them all penned up here! Signal the office, 42, and bid them send us a sergeant. This way, fellows—up Church Alley!"

With this I was down my ladder again. But my gang of savages needed no more. I could hear them rushing out of the alley as fast as they might, not one of them waiting for 24 or 47. This was lucky for me, for as it happened I was ten minutes older before I heard two patrolmen on the outside, wondering what frightened old cove had been at the pains to spring a rattle.

The moonlight shone in at the western window of the kitchen, so that as I came in I could just make out the figure of my mother, and of the girl, lying, rather than sitting, in her lap and her arms. I was not afraid to speak now, and I told my mother we were quite safe again, and she told the poor girl so. I struck a match and lighted the lamp as soon as I could. The poor, frightened creature started as I did so, and then fell on her knees at my mother's feet, took both her hands in her own, and seemed like one who begs for mercy, or, indeed, for life.

My poor, dear mother was all amazed, and her eyes were running with tears at the sight of the poor thing's terror. She kissed her again and again; she stroked her beautiful golden hair with her soft hands; she said in every word that she could think of that she was quite safe now, and must not think of being frightened any more.

But it was clear in a moment that the girl could not understand any language that we could speak. My mother tried her with a few words of German, and she smiled then; but she shook her head prettily, as if to say that she thanked her, but could not speak to her in that way either. Then she spoke eagerly in some language that we could not understand. But had it been the language of Hottentots, we should have known that she was begging my mother not to forsake her, so full of entreaty was every word and every gesture.

My dear, sweet mother lifted her at last into the easy-chair and made her lie there while she dipped some hot water from her boiler and filled a large basin in her sink. Then she led the pretty creature to it, and washed from her arms, hands, and face the blood that had hardened upon them, and looked carefully to find what her wounds were. None of them were deep, though there were ugly scratches on her beautiful arms; they were cut by glass, as I guessed then, and as we learned from her afterward. My mother was wholly prepared for all such surgery as was needed here; she put on two bandages where she thought they were needed, she plastered up the other scratches with court-plaster, and then, as if the girl understood her, she said to her, "And now, my dear child, you must come to bed; there is no danger for you more."

The poor girl had grown somewhat reassured in the comfortable little kitchen, but her terror seemed to come back at any sign of removal; she started to her feet, almost as if she were a wild creature. But I would defy any one to be afraid of my dear mother, or indeed to refuse to do what she bade, when she smiled so in her inviting way and put out her hand; and so the girl went with her, bowing to me, or dropping a sort of courtesy in her foreign fashion, as she went out of the door, and I was left to see what damage had been done to my castle by the savages, as I called them.

I had sprung the rattle none too soon; for one of these rascals, as it proved—I suppose it was the same who swore that she had not gone into the church—with some tool or other he had in his hand, had split out a bit of the fence and had pried out a part of a plank. I had done my work too well for any large piece to give way. But the moment I looked into my coal-bin I saw that something was amiss. I did not like very well to go to the outside, but I must risk something; so I took out a dark lantern which I always kept ready. Sure enough, as I say, the fellow had struck so hard and so well that he had split out a piece of board, and a little coal even had fallen upon the passage-way. I was not much displeased at this, for if he thought no nearer the truth than that he had broken into a coal-bin of the church, why, he was far enough from his mark for me. After finding this, however, I was anxious enough, lest any of them should return, not to go to bed again that night; but all was still as death, and, to tell the truth, I fell asleep in my chair. I doubt whether my mother slept, or her frightened charge.

I was at work in the passage early the next morning with some weather-stained boards I had, and before nine o'clock I had doubled all that piece of fence, from my wing where my hand-cart was to the church, and I had spiked the new boards on, which looked like old boards, as I said, with tenpenny nails; so that he would be a stout burglar who would cut through them unless he had tools for his purpose and daylight to work by. As I was gathering up my tools to go in, a coarse, brutal-looking Irishman came walking up the alley and looked round. My work was so well done, and I had been so careful to leave no chips, that even then he could not have guessed that I had been building the fence anew, though I fancied he looked at it. He seemed to want to excuse himself for being there at all, and asked me, with an oath and in a broad Irish brogue, if there were no other passage through. I had the presence of mind to say in German, "*Wollen sie sprechen Deutsch?*" and so made as if I could not understand him; and then, kneeling on the cellar-door of the church, pretended to put a key into the lock, as if I were making sure that I had made it firm.

And with that, he turned round with another oath, as if he had come out of his way, and went out of the alley, closely followed by me. I watched him as long as I dared, but as he showed no sign of going back to the alley, I at last walked round a square with my tools, and so came back to my mother and the pretty stranger.

My mother had been trying to get at her story. She made her understand a few words of German, but they talked by signs and smiles and tears and kisses much more than by words; and by this time they understood each other so well that my mother had persuaded her not to go away that day.

Nor did she go out for many days after; I will go before my story far enough to say that. She had, indeed, been horribly frightened that night, and she was as loath to go out again into the streets of New York as I should be to plunge from a safe shore into some terrible, howling ocean; or, indeed, as one who found himself safe at home would be to trust himself to the tender mercies of a tribe of cannibals.

Two such loving women as they were were not long in building up a language, especially as my mother had learned from my father and his friends, in her early life, some of the common words of German—what she called a bread-and-butter German. For our new inmate was a Swedish girl. Her story, in short, was this:—

She had been in New York but two days. On the voyage over, they had had some terrible sickness on the vessel, and the poor child's mother had died very suddenly and had been buried in the sea. Her father had died long before.

This was, as you may think, a terrible shock to her. But she had hoped and hoped for the voyage to come to an end, because there was a certain brother of hers in America whom they were to meet at their landing, and though she was very lonely on the packet-ship, in which she and her mother and a certain family of the name of Hantsen—of whom she had much to say—were the only Swedes, still she expected to find the brother almost as soon, as I may say, as they saw the land.

She felt badly enough that he did not come on board with the quarantine officer. When the passengers were brought to Castle Garden, and no brother came, she felt worse. However, with the help of the clerks there, she got off a letter to him, somewhere in Jersey, and proposed to wait as long as they would let her, till he should come.

The second day there came a man to the Garden, who said he was a Dane, but he spoke Swedish well enough. He said her brother was sick, and had sent him to find her. She was to come with her trunks, and her mother's, and all their affairs, to his house, and the same afternoon they should go to where the brother was.

Without doubt or fear she went with this man, and spent the day at a forlorn sort of hotel which she described, but which I never could find again. Toward night the man came again, and bade her take a bag, with her own change of dress, and come with him to her brother.

After a long ride through the city, they got out at a house which, thank God! was only one block from Fernando Street. And there this simple, innocent creature, as she went in, asked where her brother was, to meet only a burst of laughter from one or two coarse-looking men, and from half-a-dozen brazen-faced girls, whom she hated, she said, the minute she saw them.

Except that an old woman took off her shawl and cloak and bonnet, and took away from her the travelling things she had in her hand, nobody took any care of her but to laugh at her, and mock her if she dared say anything.

She tried to go out to the door to find even the Dane who had brought her there, but she was given to understand that he was coming again for her, and that she must wait till he came. As for her brother, there was no brother there, nor had been any. The poor girl had been trapped, and saw that she had been trapped; she had been spirited away from everybody who ever heard of her mother, and was in the clutches, as she said to my mother afterward, of a crew of devils who knew nothing of love or of mercy.

They did try to make her eat and drink—tried to make her drink champagne, or any other wine; but they had no fool to deal with. The girl did not, I think, let her captors know how desperate were her resolutions. But her eyes were wide open, and she was not going to lose any chance. She was all on the alert for her escape when, at eleven o'clock, the Dane came at last whom she had been expecting so anxiously.

The girl asked him for her brother, only to be put off by one excuse or another, and then to hear from him the most loathsome talk of his admiration, not to say his passion, for her.

They were nearly alone by this time, and he led her unresisting, as he thought, into another smaller room, brilliantly lighted, and, as she saw in a glance, gaudily furnished, with wine and fruit and cake on a side-table,—a room where they would be quite alone.

She walked simply across and looked at herself in the great mirror. Then she made some foolish little speech about her hair, and how pale she looked. Then she crossed to the sofa, and sat upon it with as tired an air as he might have expected of one who had lived through such a day. Then she looked up at him, and even smiled upon him, she said, and asked him if he would not ask them for some cold water.

The fellow turned into the passage-way, well pleased with her submission, and in the same instant the girl was at the window as if she had flown across the room.

Fool! The window was made fast, not by any moving bolt, either. It was nailed down, and it did not give a hair's-breadth to her hand.

Little cared she for that. She sat on the window-seat, which was broad enough to hold her; she braced her feet against the foot of the bedstead, which stood just near enough to her; she turned enough to bring her shoulder against the window-sash, and then with her whole force she heaved herself against the sash, and the entire window, of course, gave way.

The girl caught herself upon the blind, which swung open before her. She pulled herself free from the sill and window-seat, and dropped fearless into the street.

The fall was not long. She lighted on her feet, and ran as only fear could teach her to run. Where to, she knew not; but she thought she turned a corner before she heard any voices from behind.

Still she ran. And it was when she came to the corner of the next street that she heard for the first time the screams of pursuers.

She turned again, like a poor hunted hare as she was. But what was her running to theirs? She was passing our long fence in Fernando Street, and then for the first time she screamed for help.

It was that scream which waked me.

She saw the steeple of the church. She had a dim feeling that a church would be an asylum. So was it that she ran up our alley, to find that she was in a trap there.

And then it was that she fell against my door, that she cried twice, "Oh, my God! Oh, my God!" and that the good God who had heard her sent me to draw her in.

We had to learn her language, in a fashion, and she to learn ours, before we understood her story in this way. But at the very first my mother made out that the girl had fled from savages who meant worse than death for her. So she understood why she was so frightened at every sound, and why at first she was afraid to stay with us, yet more afraid to go.

But this passed off in a day or two. She took to my mother with a sort of eager way which showed how she must have loved her own mother, and how much she lost when she lost her. And that was one of the parts of her sad story that we understood.

No one, I think, could help loving my mother; but here was a poor, storm-tossed creature, who, I might say, had nothing else to love, seeing she had lost all trace of this brother, and here was my mother, soothing her, comforting her, dressing her wounds for her, trying to make her feel that God's world was not all wickedness; and the girl in return poured out her whole heart.

When my mother explained to her that she should not let her go away till her brother was found, then for the first time she seemed perfectly happy. She was indeed the loveliest creature I ever put my eyes on.

She was then about nineteen years old, of a delicate complexion naturally, which was now a little browned by the sea-air. She was rather tall than otherwise, but her figure was so graceful that I think you never thought her tall. Her eyes were perhaps deep-set, and of that strange gray which I have heard it said the goddesses in the Greek poetry had. Still, when she was sad, one saw the less of all this. It was not till she forgot her grief for the instant in the certainty that she might rest with my mother, so that her whole face blazed with joy, that I first knew what the perfect beauty of a perfect woman was.

Her name, it seemed, was Frida,—a name made from the name of one of the old goddesses among the Northmen, the same from whom our day Friday is named. She is the half-sister of Thor, from whom Thursday is named, and the daughter of Odin, from whom Wednesday is named.

I knew little of all this then, but I did not wonder when I read afterward that this northern goddess was the Goddess of Love, the friend of song, the most beautiful of all their divinities,—queen of spring and light and everything lovely.

But surely never any one took fewer of the airs of a goddess than our Frida did while she was with us. She would watch my mother, as if afraid that she should put her hand to a gridiron or a tin dipper. She gave her to understand, in a thousand pretty ways, that she should be her faithful, loving, and sincere servant. If she would only show her what to do, she would work for her as a child that loved her. And so indeed she did. My dear mother would laugh and say she was quite a fine lady now, for Frida would not let her touch broom nor mop, skimmer nor dusting-cloth.

The girl would do anything but go out upon an errand. She could not bear to see the other side of the fence. What she thought of it all I do not know. Whether she thought it was the custom in America for young men to live shut up with their mothers in inclosures of half an acre square, or whether she thought we two made some peculiar religious order, whose rules provided that one woman and one man should live together in a convent or monastery of their own, or whether she supposed half New York was made up, as Marco Polo found Pekin, of cottages or of gardens, I did not know, nor did I much care. I could see that here was provided a companion for my mother, who was else so lonely, and I very soon found that she was as much a companion for me.

So soon as we could understand her at all, I took the name of her brother and his address. When he wrote last he was tending a saw-mill at a place about seven miles away from Tuckahoe, in Jersey. But he said he was going to leave there at once, so that they need not write there. He sent the money for their passage, and promised, as I said, to meet them at New York.

This was a poor clew at the best. But I put a good face on it, and promised her I would find him if he could be found. And I spared no pains. I wrote to the postmaster at Tuckahoe, and to a minister I heard of there. I inquired of the Swedish consuls in New York and Philadelphia. Indeed, in the end, I went to Tuckahoe myself, with her, to inquire. But this was long after. However, I may say here, once for all, to use an old phrase of my mother's, we never found "hide nor hair" of him. And although this grieved Frida, of course, yet it came on her gradually, and, as she had never seen him to remember him, it was not the same loss as if they had grown up together.

Meanwhile that first winter was, I thought, the pleasantest I had ever known in my life. I did not have to work very hard now, for my business was rather the laying out work for my men, and sometimes a nice job which needed my hand on my lathe at home, or in some other delicate affair that I could bring home with me.

We were teaching Frida English, my mother and I, and she and I made a great frolic of her teaching me Swedish. I would bring home Swedish newspapers and stories for her, and we would puzzle them out together,—she as much troubled to find the English word as I to find out the Swedish. Then she sang like a bird, when she was about her household work, or when she sat sewing for my mother, and she had not lived with us a fortnight before she began to join us on Sunday evenings in the choruses of the Methodist hymns which my mother and I sang together. So then we made her sing Swedish hymns to us. And, before she knew it, the great tears would brim over her deep eyes, and would run down in pearls upon her cheek. Nothing set her to thinking of her old home as those Sunday evenings did. Of a Sunday evening we could make her go out with us to church sometimes. Not but then she would half cover her face with a vail, so afraid was she that we might meet the Dane. But I told her that the last place we should find him at would be at church on Sunday evening.

I have come far in advance of my story, that I might make any one who reads this life of mine to understand how naturally and simply this poor lost bird nestled down into our quiet life, and how the house that was built for two proved big enough for three. For I made some new purchases now, and fitted up the little middle chamber for Frida's own use. We had called it the "spare chamber" before, in joke. But now my mother fitted pretty curtains to it, and other hangings, without Frida's knowledge. I had a square of carpet made up at the warehouse for the middle of the floor, and, by making her do one errand and another in the corner of the garden, one pleasant afternoon in November, we had it all prettily fitted up for her room before she knew it. And a great gala we made of it when she came in from gathering the seeds of the calystegia, which she had been sent for.

She looked like a northern Flora, as she came in, with her arms all festooned by the vines she had been pulling down. And when my mother made her come out to the door she had never seen opened before, and led her in, and told her that this pretty chamber was all her own, the pretty creature flushed crimson red at first, and then her quick tears ran over, and she fell on my mother's neck, and kissed her as if she would never be done. And then she timidly held her hand out to me, too, as I stood in the doorway, and said, in her slow, careful English,—

"And you, too—and you, too. I must tank you both, also, especially. You are so good—so good to de poor lost girl!" That was a very happy evening.

But, as I say, I have gone ahead of my story. For before we had these quiet evenings we were fated to have many anxious ones and one stormy one.

The very first day that Frida was with us, I felt sure that the savages would make another descent upon us. They had heard her scream, that was certain. They knew she had not passed them, that was certain. They knew there was a coal-bin on the other side of our fence, that was certain. They would have reason enough for being afraid to have her at large, if, indeed, there were no worse passion than fear driving some of them in pursuit of her. I could not keep out of my mind the beastly look of the Irishman, who asked me, with such an ugly leer on his face, if there were no passage through. Not that I told either of the two women of my fears. But, all the same, I did not undress myself for a week, and sat in the great easy-chair in our kitchen through the whole of every night, waiting for the least sound of alarm.

Next to the savages, I had always lived in fear of being discovered in my retreat by the police, who would certainly think it strange to find a man and his mother living in a shed, without any practicable outside door, in what they called a vacant lot.

But I have read of weak nations in history which were fain to call upon one neighbor whom they did not like, to protect them against another whom they liked less. I made up my mind, in like wise, to go round to the police-station nearest me.

And so, having dressed myself in my black coat, and put on a round hat and gloves, I bought me a Malacca walking-stick, such as was then in fashion, and called upon the captain in style. I told him I lived next the church, and that, on such and such a night, there was a regular row among roughs, and that several of them went storming up the alley in a crowd. I said, "Although your men were there as quick as they could come, these fellows had all gone before they came." But then I explained that I had seen a fellow hanging about the alley in the daytime, who seemed to be there for no good; that there was a hand-cart kept there by a workman, who seemed to be an honest fellow, and, perhaps, all they wanted was to steal that; that, if I could, I would warn him. But, meanwhile, I said, I had come round to the station to give the warning of my suspicions, that, if my rattle was heard again, the patrolmen might know what was in the wind.

The captain was a good deal impressed by my make-up and by the ease of my manner. He affected to be perfectly well acquainted with me, although we had never happened to meet at the Century Club or at the Union League. I confirmed the favorable impression I had made by leaving my card which I had had handsomely engraved: "MR. ROBINSON CRUSOE." With my pencil I added my down-town address, where, I said, a note or telegram would find me.

I was not a day too soon with my visit to this gentleman. That very night, after my mother and Frida had gone to bed, as I sat in my easy-chair, there came over me one of those strange intimations which I have never found it safe to disregard. Sometimes it is of good, and sometimes of bad. This time it made me certain that all was not well. To relieve my fears I lifted my ladder over the wall, and dropped it in the alley. I swung myself down, and carried it to the very end of the alley, to the place where I had dragged poor Frida in. The moon fell on the fence opposite ours. My wing-fence and hand-cart were all in shade. But everything was safe there.

Again I chided myself for my fears, when, as I looked up the alley to the street, I saw a group of four men come in stealthily. They said not a word, but I could make out their forms distinctly against the houses opposite.

I was caught in my own trap!

Not quite! They had not seen me, for I was wholly in shadow. I stepped quickly in at my own slide. I pushed it back and bolted it securely, and with my heart in my mouth, I waited at my hole of observation. In a minute more they were close around me, though they did not suspect I was so near.

They, also, had a dark-lantern, and, I thought, more than one. They spoke in low tones; but, as they had no thought they had a hearer quite so near, I could hear all they said.

"I tell you it was this side, and this is the side I heard their deuced psalm-singing, day before yesterday."

"What if he did hear psalm-singing? Are you going to break into a man's garden because he sings psalms? I came here to find out where the girl went to; and now you talk of psalm-singing and coal-bins." This from another, whose English was poor, and in whom I fancied I heard the Dane. It was clear enough that he spoke sense, and a sort of doubt fell on the whole crew; but speaker No. 1, with a heavy crowbar he had, smashes into my pine wall, as I have a right to call it now, with a force which made the splinters fly.

"I should think we were all at Niblo's," said a man of slighter build, "and that we were playing Humpty Dumpty. Because a girl flew out of a window, you think a fence opened to take her in. Why should she not go through a door?" and he kicked with his foot upon the heavy sloping cellar-door of the church, which just rose a little from the pavement. It was the doorway which they used there when they took in their supply of coal. The moon fell full on one side of it. To my surprise it was loose and gave way.

"Here is where the girl flew to, and here is where Bully Bigg, the donkey, let her slip out of his fingers. I knew he was a fool, but I did not know he was such a fool," said the Dane (if he were the Dane).

I will not pretend to write down the oaths and foul words which came in between every two of the words I have repeated.

"Fool yourself!" replied the Bully; "and what sort of a fool is the man who comes up a blind alley, looking after a girl that will not kiss him when he bids her?"

"Anyway," put in another of the crew, who had just now lifted the heavy cellar-door, "other people may find it handy to hop down here when the 'beaks' are too near them. It's a handy place to know of, in a dark night, if the dear deacons do choose to keep it open for a poor psalm-singing tramp, who has no chance at the station-house. Here, Lopp, you are the tallest—jump in and tell us what is there"; and at this moment the Dane caught sight of my unfortunate ladder, lying full in the moonlight. I could see him seize it, and run to the doorway with it, with a deep laugh, and some phrase of his own country talk, which I did not understand.

"The deacons are very good," said the savage who had lifted the cellar-door. "They make everything handy for us poor fellows."

And though he had not planted the ladder, he was the first to run down, and called for the rest to follow. The Dane was second, Lopp was third, and "The Bully," as the big rascal seemed to be called by distinction, was the fourth.

I saw him disappear from my view, with a mixture of wonder and terror which I will not describe. I seized my light overcoat, which always hung in the passage. I flung open my sliding-door, and shut it again behind me. I looked into the black of the cellar to see the reflections from their distant lanterns, and, without a sound, I drew up my ladder. Then I ran to the head of the alley, and sounded my rattle as I would have sounded the trumpet for a charge in battle. The officers joined me in one moment.

"I am the man who spoke to the captain about these rowdies. Four of them are in the cellar of the church yonder now."

"Do you know who?"

"One they called Lopp, and one they called Bully Bigg," said I. "I do not know the others' names."

The officers were enraptured.

I led them, and two other patrolmen who joined us, to the shelter of my wing-wall. In a few minutes the head of the Dane appeared, as he was lifted from below. With an effort and three or four oaths, he struggled out upon the ground, to be seized and gagged the moment he stepped back. With varying fortunes, Bigg and Lopp emerged, and were seized and handcuffed in turn. The fourth surrendered on being summoned.

What followed comes into the line of daily life and the morning newspaper so regularly that I need not describe it. Against the Dane it proved that endless warrants could be brought immediately. His lair of stolen baggage and other property was unearthed, and countless sufferers claimed their own. I was able to recover Frida's and her mother's possessions—the locks on the trunks still unbroken. The Dane himself would have been sent to the Island on I know not how many charges, but that the Danish minister asked for him that he might be hanged in Denmark, and he was sent and hanged accordingly.

Lopp was sent to Sing-Sing for ten years, and has not yet been pardoned.

Bigg and Cordon were sent to Blackwell's Island for three years each. And so the land had peace for that time.

That winter, as there came on one and another idle alarm that Frida's brother might be heard from, my heart sank with the lowest terror lest she should go away. And in the spring I told her that if she went away I was sure I should die. And the dear girl looked down, and looked up, and said she thought—she thought she should, too. And we told my mother that we had determined that Frida should never go away while we stayed there. And she approved.

So I wrote a note to the minister of the church which had protected us so long, and one night we slid the board carefully, and all three walked round, fearless of the Dane, and Frida and I were married.

   *   *   *   *   *

It was more than three years after, when I received, by one post, three letters, which gave us great ground for consultation. The first was from my old friend and patron, the Spaniard. He wrote to me from Chicago, where he, in his turn, had fallen in with a crew of savages, who had stripped him of all he had, under the pretext of a land-enterprise they engaged him in, and had left him without a real, as he said. He wanted to know if I could not find him some clerkship, or even some place as janitor, in New York.

The second letter was from old Mr. Henry in Philadelphia, who had always employed me after my old master's death. He said that the fence around the lot in Ninety-ninth Avenue might need some repairs, and he wished I would look at it. He was growing old, he said, and he did not care to come to New York. But the Fordyce heirs would spend ten years in Europe.

The third letter was from Tom Grinnell.

34

I wrote to Mr. Henry that I thought he had better let me knock up a little office, where a keeper might sleep, if necessary; that there was some stuff with which I could put up such an office, and that I had an old friend, a Spaniard, who was an honest fellow, and if he might have his bed in the office, would take gratefully whatever his services to the estate proved worth. He wrote me by the next day's mail that I might engage the Spaniard and finish the office. So I wrote to the Spaniard and got a letter from him, accepting the post provided for him. Then I wrote to Tom Grinnell.

The last day we spent at our dear old home, I occupied myself in finishing the office as Friend Henry bade me. I made a "practicable door," which opened from the passage on Church Alley. Then I loaded my hand-cart with my own chest, and took it myself, in my working clothes, to the Vanderbilt Station, where I took a brass check for it.

I could not wait for the Spaniard, but I left a letter for him, giving him a description of the way I managed the goats, and directions to milk and fatten them, and to make both butter and cheese.

At half-past ten, a "crystal," as those cabs were then called, came to the corner of Fernando Street and Church Alley, and so we drove to the station. I left the key of the office, directed to the Spaniard, in the hands of the baggage-master.

When I took leave of my castle, as I called it, I carried with me for relics the great straw hat I had made, my umbrella, and one of my parrots; also I forgot not to take the money I formerly mentioned, which had lain by me so long useless that it was grown rusty and tarnished, and could scarcely pass for money till it had been a little rubbed and handled. With these relics, and with my wife's and mother's baggage and my own chest, we arrived at our new home.

ALIF-LAILA.

THE ORIGIN OF THE "SERIAL."

The monthly magazine, as known to our Western civilization, dates, of course, from a period this side of the re-invention of printing in Europe, or of what Bishop Whately wisely calls the introduction of paper in the West. Our sets of monthlies, bi-monthlies, and semi-monthlies only run back a hundred or two years, therefore—to the joy of librarians, to whom, be it confessed, they bring misery untold.

But in the East, where printing has existed so long that the memory of man goes not to the contrary, it is almost impossible to say how far back was the introduction of the monthly literary magazine. This publication was accompanied with certain advantages and certain disadvantages, which sprang from the peculiarities of the Eastern calendar. The Eastern month being lunar, the magazine, if accuracy were consulted, had to be issued once in twenty-nine days, twelve hours, and forty-four minutes. On the other hand, the people of the East are less exacting or precise than we are in their estimates of time; and in the long run, if they had thirteen monthlies in one year, and twelve in each of the next two years, it generally proved that subscribers were satisfied.

There is a story of two of these early magazines—universally known through the East, where, indeed, it is told in many exaggerated and impossible forms —which is worth repeating for Western readers not yet familiar with it. It gives both instruction and warning in an age in which every boy in college, and every girl in a "female seminary," regards magazine-writing as the chief end of man and of woman,—an age in which editors are feeling round, somewhat blindly, to know what their rights may be, or whether, in fact, they have any rights, which is doubtful. The story simply told, without any of the absurd adornments which are put upon it in the East, teaches all men how some of the most difficult editorial questions were decided there, and what are the delicate relations between contributors and the public.

Far back in the period of mythical history in the East two brothers, men of spirit, tact, shrewdness, and literary culture, conducted at the same time two monthly magazines. The offices of publication were so far from each other, and the "constituencies" were so different, that the two journals did not in the least interfere with each other. Those were in the happy days when there were no mails; and each magazine had its own staff and its own contributors, the one set skilled in the language and literature of Tartary, and the other in those of India. Though the two brothers loved each other, they seldom exchanged letters, and the chosen contributors of one journal never sent articles to the other.

One of these magazines, called the "Friend of the City," in their queer Eastern way, was published at Delhi. The other, called the "King of the Age," was published at Samarcand. Each of them achieved great popularity, and, by virtue of its popularity, great power. At Delhi, in particular, the editor became the real controlling power in the city, and in what we call the kingdom. Not but what there was some kind of a sachem or mikado, who in after ages would have been called a sultan or an emperor, who did not edit the magazine, but was kept for or by his sins in a certain prison, which he called a palace, which stood where Shah Jehan long after built his magnificent abode. But this poor dog of a mikado had nothing to do with the real government. He had to put his seal to a good many documents, and he had to settle a horrible mess of quarrels among his servants and harem people every day; and sometimes he had the bore of turning out in the hot sun, with umbrellas and elephants and bands of music, and so on, to receive some foreign embassy. This he called reigning, and a very stupid life it was, and very hard work did it bring upon him. But all the fun of command, all the real disposition of the forces of Delhi and that country, and all the comfort of life which comes from success and the "joy of eventful living," these came, not to this poor shah, mogul, sultan, emperor, or sachem, or whatever you choose to call him, but to the editor of the "Friend of the City." He drove his span of horses when he chose and as he chose, he sent the army where he chose when he chose, and he dictated the terms of the treaties with the foreign powers. All this he did because he had a large subscription list and he edited well.

With similar success, though with some difference in form, his younger brother edited the "King of the Age" at distant Samarcand. Now you ought to know, dear reader, what I am sorry to say you do not know, that Samarcand is far, far away from Delhi. It is more than a thousand miles, were a carrier-dove flying to his love in Delhi from his cage in Samarcand; and when you come to tedious travelling by camels and horses and asses—why, there are rivers and mountains between, and the ways, such as they are, turn hither and thither, so that the journey is two thousand miles or more. All the same, the editor of the "Friend of the City" dearly loved his brother who edited the "King of the Age"; and after they had been parted twenty years, he felt so strong a desire to see this brother that he directed his chief assistant editor to repair to him at Samarcand and to bring him.

Having taken the advice of this sub-editor, who was a more practical person than he was, he gave orders to prepare handsome presents, such as horses adorned with costly jewels, and mamelukes and beautiful virgins, and the most expensive stuffs of India. He then wrote a letter to his brother, in which he told him how eager he was to see him; and having sealed it and given it to the sub-editor, together with the presents, he bade him strain his nerves and tuck up his skirts, and go and return as quickly as possible. The sub-editor answered, "I hear, and I obey." He packed his baggage and made ready his provisions in three days, and on the fourth day he departed and went toward the wastes and the mountains. He travelled night and day. The different newsagents in the provinces where he stopped came forth to meet him with costly presents and gifts of gold and silver, and accounts of sales and orders for back numbers and bound volumes, and each news-agent accompanied the sub-editor one day's journey. Thus he continued until he approached the city of Samarcand, when he sent forward a messenger to the editor of the "King of the Age" to inform him of his approach. The messenger entered the city, inquired the way to the office, and introducing himself to the editor, kissed the ground before him, and acquainted him with the approach of his brother's sub-editor. On this the editor ordered all his staff, with the proof-readers and publishers, to go forth a day's journey to meet him, and they did so. And when they met him, they welcomed him and walked by his stirrups till they returned into the city. The messenger from Delhi then delivered his chief's letter. The Samarcand editor took it, read it, and understood its contents. "But," said he to the messenger, "I will not go till I have entertained thee three days." He therefore lodged him in a palace befitting his rank, accommodated all his suite in tents, and appointed all things requisite in food and drink, and for three days they feasted. His New-Year's number was just printed, and having got that off his hands, on the fourth day he equipped himself for the journey, and collected presents suitable to his brother's dignity.

Having completed these preparations, he left the charge of the magazine with his chief of staff, and set out for his visit to his brother. As is the custom in the East, the caravan encamped a mile from the city to make sure that nothing was forgotten. It occurred to the Samarcand brother, after his evening meal, that it would be well to take with him an early copy of the New-Year's number in advance to his brother, as they were not yet delivered to the trade. He mounted his horse, therefore, and rode back to the city, and to save himself from going to the office, he stopped near the gates, at the house of one of his chief contributors—a young lady of great promise, whose reputation had been manufactured, indeed, by the "King of the Age"—to ask her, for the "early copy" which had been sent to her because she had some verses in it.

What did he see as he entered the house but that this false woman was giving a sealed letter to a negro slave. He seized it, he tore it open, and found that it was a copy of verses which she had written and addressed to the "Fountain of Light," which was the rival magazine in Samarcand. On beholding this, the world became black before his eyes. He said to himself, "If this happens when I have not departed from the city, what will not this vile woman do while I am sojourning with my brother?" He then drew his cimeter and cut off her head, as she fell at his knees for pardon. He took from her table the early copy of the "King of the Age," gave orders for departure, and journeyed to the city of

Delhi.

As they approached Delhi, the "Friend of the City," or the editor of that journal, came out to meet them, and welcomed his brother with the utmost delight. He then ordered that the city should be decorated for the occasion. But the mind of his brother was distracted by reflections upon the conduct of his favorite contributor. Excessive grief took possession of him, and his countenance became sallow and his frame emaciated. His brother observed these symptoms of a mind ill at ease, and asked him the cause. "O my brother," he replied, "I have an inward wound"; but he explained not to him the cause. His host then proposed a great press excursion on the Jumna, which he hoped might cheer his brother's mind. But after all the preparations had been made, he was destined to suffer disappointment, his brother being so ill that the party proceeded without him.

After they had gone, the poor sufferer from Samarcand sat in his beautiful apartment in his brother's palace, and to divert his mind, looked out into the garden. Scarcely was the excursion party gone, when a gay, laughing party of young men and women came into the garden, whom he recognized at once as being the contributors to his brother's magazine, all of whom had been introduced to him at a collation the day before. He was interested to see their proceedings. They entertained themselves in the garden; and the favorite contributor of all, a lady celebrated through India for her short stories, sat down by a fountain, clapped her hands, and cried, "Masoud! Masoud!" Now Masoud was the editor of the "Pearl of Wit," which was an upstart magazine, the hated rival of the "Friend of the City." In a moment he came in, led by two mamelukes, who made prostrations before him; and he bowed to the chief contributor, and sat at her feet. Then she drew from her pocket a little roll of vellum, and read to him and to all the others a short story of only six thousand words. And all the contributors applauded, some from sympathy and some to conceal their jealousy. But Masoud applauded most of all, and took the roll, and hung around her neck a necklace of diamonds. Then all the other contributors read articles in turn; and Masoud took an article from each, and to each he gave either a purse of gold or a bracelet or a diamond, according to the reputation before the public of each contributor. Now all these reputations had been made by the advertising clerk of the "Friend of the City."

When, therefore, the Samarcand editor saw from his window these shameless proceedings, his heart warmed gladly within him. "By Allah!" he exclaimed, "my affliction is lighter than this affliction!" His grief was soothed, and he no longer abstained from food and drink.

And so it fell out that when, after five days, his brother returned from the excursion, he was delighted to find that his brother guest was cheerful and well. His face had recovered its color, and he ate with appetite. "O my brother," he cried, "how is this change? Acquaint me with thy condition." Then his brother took him on one side, away from the staff, from the mamelukes and the publishers, and told him all. The Delhi editor could not believe the tale. But the next day he made as if he would go on an excursion with the Board of Trade; and no sooner had the party left the city than he returned to his palace in disguise, and then, looking from the window as his brother had done, he saw a like sight: the contributors were all reading their articles, and selling them to Masoud and other editors of rival magazines.

As soon as the editor saw this, he wrote a note to the chief contributor, and asked her to call at the office the next day. So soon as she entered, he charged her with her guilt; and before the miserable creature could reply, he drew his cimeter and cut off her head. He then sent shorter notes to the lesser contributors; and as each one entered the office, he explained briefly that he knew all, and, with his own hand, beheaded him. He then ordered the porters and janitors to throw the heads and bodies into the Jumna, and, with his brother's assistance, he called in a new circle of new contributors, and made up the next number of the "Friend of the City" from their poems and articles. The director of advertisements and of press criticisms manufactured reputations for them all, and the number was pronounced the most brilliant number of the "Friend of the City" which had ever been published.

Then the editor sent advance copies to each of these contributors, and asked them to call at the office the next morning. As each one called, the editor drew his cimeter and cut off the contributor's head. He then called the porters and janitors, and bade them throw the carcasses and heads into the Jumna, and proceeded to make up the next number. And thus he did for three years.

As the third year passed, however, the assistant editors began to observe that there was a certain difficulty in collecting poems and articles. Nay, it was even whispered that in the publication office they feared that the magazine was losing popularity. The rumors from the publication office were not often permitted to exhale in the editorial rooms. But still there was a suspicion that from the homes of the authors, who had been cut short so summarily, there was going out a sort of public opinion unfavorable to the renewal of subscriptions. As for authors, for some time they presented themselves freely. Each poet and each story-writer was quite sure that her communication was so much better than anything which had ever been written before that they all moved up to the fatal edge of publication with serenity, each quite sure that for herself the rule would be reversed, and each quite sure that the others deserved decapitation. But, as has been said, after three years the steady supply of articles was a little checked, perhaps because a rumor was put in circulation by the conductors of the "Pearl of Wit" that the editor of the "Friend of the City" was crazy, and could not if he would, and would not if he could, tell a bad article from a good one.

All these rumors and contingencies made the position of the sub-editor very uncomfortable as the third year drew to a close. He had to make up each number all the same, and he had to direct the chief of the advertisements how to make the reputations of the authors. But really the authors were so short-lived now that the reputations were scarcely worth the making.

Of this remarkable man the name unfortunately is lost. But, happily for literature and for posterity, he had two remarkable daughters, of whom the eldest has won an extraordinary reputation in the East, where she stands, indeed, at the very head of literature. At the period with which this history deals she was young and beautiful. She had a courage above her sex, remarkable penetration, and genius unbounded. She had read everything, and her memory was so wonderful that of all she had read she forgot nothing. She had studied history, philosophy, medicine, and the arts, and her verses were acknowledged to be better than those of the most distinguished poets of her time. As has been said, her beauty was ravishing, and her amiability and her virtue rivalled her wit, her memory, her prudence, her accomplishments, and her personal loveliness.

One day, when the sub-editor had white paper before him, wondering how he should make up the "schedule" for his next number, this lovely girl came to him and said, "Papa, grant me a boon!" and she kissed him.

And he said, "A thousand, my darling."

"Though they should cost you the half of your kingdom, papa?"

"Though they should cost me the whole, my darling," said the fond father rashly.

The girl clapped her hands and cried, "Victory! victory! Papa, I want to write the first article for the next number of the 'Friend of the City.'"

Oh, how agonized was her poor father! How he begged her to release him from his fatal promise! but in vain. The girl was determined. She had her father's word, and she would not let him go.

"Dear child," he said, "have you lost your senses? You know that the chief cuts off the head of each contributor as soon as she has received the advanced copy of the magazine. Do you really ask me to offer you to the knife?"

"Yes, papa," said the brave girl; "I know all the danger that I run, and it does not deter me. If I die, my death will be glorious. If I live, I save my country."

And at last the wretched father, driven to a partial consent by his daughter's firmness, went to the editor-in-chief with the schedule of the number for his approval, and showed to him that the first article on the fatal list, namely,

"THE TRAVELLING MERCHANT,"

was

"BY SCHEHEREZADE."

The editor knew the name full well, and he knew that the author was the sub-editor's daughter.

"Dog," said he, "do you suppose that because I am fond of you and use you, I shall spare your cursed house more than any other house in Delhi?"

The poor sub-editor, all in tears, said that he had no such hope.

"Be not deceived," said the editor. "When you bring to me your daughter Scheherezade's article, you take her life with your own hands."

"Sir," said the sub-editor, "I hear and I obey. My heart will break, but I shall obey you. Nature will murmur, but I know my place, and you will see that the proofs are well read and that my hands do not flinch." The editor accepted his promise, and bade him bring the article when he pleased.

Quite in time for the first or illustrated form, the sub-editor brought in the article, with a series of spirited illustrations, drawn on the block by Dinarzade, the sister of the virgin martyr Scheherezade. This celebrated article has never been fully printed in Western journals till now, although it has attained great celebrity all over the world, and has often been printed in abridged forms. The following is a more complete and correct version of it than we have found elsewhere:—

THE TRAVELLING MERCHANT.

Once upon a time there was a rich merchant, wonderfully successful in his dealings, who had great store of goods of all sorts, of money also, and of women, children, and all sorts of slaves, as well as of houses, warehouses, and lands. And he had this wealth not only at home, but in all the countries of the world. He had to make journeys sometimes, so that he might see his factors and correspondents face to face. And once, when he was obliged to go and collect some money, he took his scrip or travel-bag, and packed in it some biscuit and some dates of Mecca for provision for the journey, because he would have in some places to pass over deserts. And so he mounted his horse and set out upon his journey. God gave him good success in his travelling. He came prosperously to the place he sought, he finished his business prosperously, and prosperously he set out upon his return.

After he had travelled three days toward home, the fourth day was very hot. And the merchant was so much distressed by the heat that he turned aside into a garden by the wayside to rest himself under the shade of some trees he saw there. He made his resting place under the shade of a large nut-tree, he fastened his horse so that he could not run, and then opening his scrip, he took out one or two biscuits and a few dates to make a meal. He ate the biscuits and the dates, and threw the date-stones right and left upon the ground. Then, having satisfied himself with his frugal repast, he stood up and washed himself, and then knelt down and said his prayers.

He had not finished his prayers, but was still upon his knees, when he saw before him an immense genie, so large that while his feet were on the ground, his head was in the clouds, and so old that he was white with age. He held in his hand a long drawn sword, and before the merchant could move, the genie cried out to him,—

"Stand up, that I may kill you with this sword, as you have killed my son!"

When the merchant heard these words of horror he was terrified by them as much as he had been at the sight of the monster; but in the midst of his terror he stammered out, "O my lord, what is my crime? why do you kill me?"

Then the genie replied again, "I will kill you, as you have killed my son."

Then the merchant said, "Who has killed your son?"

And the genie answered, "You."

"O my lord," said the poor merchant, "I never saw your son, and I do not know who he is."

But the genie said, "You have killed him."

Then the merchant said, "My lord, by the living Allah, I have not killed him. How and where and when did I kill him?"

The genie answered him, "Did you not lie down when you came into the garden? Did you not take dates out of your travel-bag, did you not eat the dates, and did you not throw the stones about, some on the left side and some on the right?"

"It is true, my lord," said the merchant; "I did as you say."

"Very well," said the genie, "and so you killed my son; for my son was passing by just then, and as you threw the date-stones, one of them struck him and killed him. Does not the law say, 'Whoso killeth another, shall be killed in turn'?"

"Verily, this is the law," said the merchant; "but indeed, indeed, my lord, I did not kill your son; or, if I killed him, I call upon Allah to witness, without Whom is no might and no wisdom, that I did it unwittingly. Forgive me, my lord, oh, forgive me if I have done this thing!"

"No," said the genie; "surely you must die."

So saying, he seized the merchant and threw him upon the ground. Then he lifted his great sword into the air again and held it ready to strike. The poor merchant thought of his home and family, of his wives and his little ones. He thought he had not a moment more to live, and he shed such floods of tears that his clothes were wet with the moisture.

He cried again, "There is no power nor might but with the infinite Allah alone!" and then he repeated the following verses:—

> "Time knows two days:
> Of one the face is bright and clear;
> Of one the face is dark and drear.
>
> "Life has two sides:
> One is as warm and glad as light;
> One is as cold and black as night.
>
> "Time fooled with me:
> His flattering fingers soothed with magic spell,
> Just while his lying kiss was luring me to hell.
>
> "Who sneers at me?
> Are not the trees that feel the tempest's blow
> The stately trees of pride that highest grow?
>
> "Come sail with me:
> See floating corpses on the topmost waves;
> The precious pearls are hid in secret caves.
>
> "See the eclipse!
> A thousand stars unquenched forever blaze;
> But sun and moon must hide their brighter rays.
>
> "I looked for fruit:
> On branches green and fresh no fruit I found;
> I plucked the fruit from branches sere and browned.
>
> "Night smiled on me!
> Because I saw the diamonds in the sky,
> Poor fool! I had forgot that death was nigh."

When the merchant had finished these verses, and had wept to his heart's content, the genie, who had waited through it all, said, "It is enough; now I must kill you."

"What!" said the merchant, "will nothing change you?"

"Nothing," said the genie. "You must die."
TO BE CONTINUED.

These last words were emblazoned in a beautiful scroll of Dinarzade's most perfect designing.

The editor of the "Friend of the City" was not accustomed, himself, to read manuscripts, proofs, or revises, unless the articles were his own. He first saw the articles of the sub-editor and contributors in plate-proof. When the plate-proofs of this number were brought to him he began at once on the story of the merchant. He read it with unaffected, not to say unwonted, interest. When he turned the last page, he said to himself, "However will she wind it up in so few lines?" And when he came to the masterpiece of Scheherezade's success and of Dinarzade's art, he laid down the sheets with a mingled feeling not easily described. His cruelty was foiled. But of that he thought little. His curiosity was piqued. A jaded editor of twenty-three years' experience was curious for a *dénouement*. But of this he thought little. For not one moment did he think of taking the author's blood. He saw too clearly the future of the magazine. In short, every other emotion sank within him before the profound awe which overwhelmed his being. The editor looked down the ages. He saw that his magazine might last forever. For in that series of plate-proofs the SERIAL was born.

From that moment the position of the lovely Scheherezade and her accomplished sister Dinarzade on that magazine was secure. That single serial ran twenty-seven years, through one thousand and one numbers, and was known through the East as "Alif-Laila." Long before it ended, other serials had been begun, and no citizen of Delhi or the neighborhood ever subscribed for the "Friend of the City" but he continued his subscription for generation after generation.

The tales of Scheherezade have been collected, as is well known, in endless editions, and translated into all languages. The languages of the East are so little understood that the names of the magazines have in time been transferred to the two editors. The "Friend of the City" in Arabic is "Shahriar," and that name in varied spelling is generally given to the editor of that print. His brother, by a similar oversight, is usually called "Shahzeban," which word means the "King of the Age."

But these names are forgotten, as they should be. The name which is remembered is that of the lovely and virtuous Scheherezade, the savior of her country, who, to her other titles to the gratitude of men, adds this,—that she invented the Serial.

A CIVIL SERVANT.

President Madison was fond of telling the story of a visit made to him by one of his supporters. After due introductory discussion of the weather and the state of parties, the voter explained to the President that he had called upon him to ask for the office of Chief Justice of the United States.

Mr. Madison was a little surprised; but, with that ready tact which he had brought from his diplomatic experience, he concealed his astonishment. He took down the volume which contained the Constitution of the United States, and explained to this Mr. Swearingin—if that were his name—that the judges held office on the tenure of good behavior, and that Judge Marshall, then the ornament of the bench, could not be removed to make place for him.

Mr. Swearingin received the announcement quietly; and, after a moment, said he thought he should like to be Secretary of State.

The President said that that was undoubtedly a place where a man could do good service to the country; but that Monroe, like Mr. Swearingin and himself, was a Virginian; and he did not like to remove him.

"Then," said Mr. Swearingin, "I will be Secretary of the Treasury."

Unfortunately, the President said, the present incumbent was a Pennsylvanian: it was necessary to conciliate Pennsylvania; and he could not remove him.

"Then," said Mr. Swearingin, "I think I will go abroad. I should like to go to France."

"Do you speak French?" asked the President kindly.

"No, no; I speak nothing but Old Dominion English,—good enough for me, Mr. President."

"Yes, yes; and for me. But I don't think it will do to send you to the Mounseers, unless you can speak their language."

"Then I'll go to England."

"Ah, Mr. Swearingin, that will never do! King George might remember how often your father snapped his rifle at Lord Cornwallis."

So Europe was exhausted. And Mr. Swearingin fell back on one and another collectorship, naval office, district-attorneyship; but for each application, the astute President had his reply.

"I think, then, Mr. President, I will be postmaster at our office at home."

Mr. Madison had forgotten where that was; but, learning that it was at Slate Creek, Four Corners, Botetourt County, Virginia, he sent for the register. Alas! it proved that the office was in the hands of one of Morgan's veterans. Impossible to remove him!

"Truly, Mr. Madison," said Mr. Swearingin, "I am obliged to you for your attention to my case. I see the difficulties that surround you. Now, seeing you cannot give me the chief justice's place, nor Mr. Monroe's, nor the Treasury, nor any of those others, don't you think you could give me a pair of *old leather breeches?*"

Mr. Madison thought he could,—did better; gave him an order on his tailor for the breeches; and Mr. Swearingin went happily on his way.

I have changed the name in this story, but tell it much as Mr. Madison told it. Something of that kind has happened every day in Washington, from 1800 to 1880. And it is of the career of one of these very civil servants of the state, who are so easily pleased if only you give them something which they have never earned, that I now am writing. I am by no means sure that our hero is not the grandson of the very man whom, by a pair of leather breeches, James Madison made happy.

The first epoch of his life is the great success, as his young friends thought it, when, before he was of age, he received an appointment as clerk in the War Department in Washington. It was then that he entered the "Civil Service," and became a "civil servant" of the United States. Why was he appointed? Why? Because there was nothing else for him to do. He had grown up shiftlessly, the oldest son of a widow, who had not a firm hand enough to keep him at school. He threw his Latin Grammar into the fire the day it was bought for him, and refused to go to college. One of his uncles offered him a farm at the West; but he did not choose to be a farmer: he said he thought he would rather be a gentleman. The same prejudice interfered with his being apprenticed to learn the printer's trade or the painter's or the carriage-builder's, or any of the other methods by which hand-laborers subdue the world; so an effort had been made, with a good deal of solicitation to back it, to put him into a wholesale importing house. But it turned out, the first day, that his figures were so dubious that no one could tell by his memoranda whether he had counted two hundred and fifteen bales of gunny cloth or

2,015. And when, on the second day, he gave to a teamster an order for two bundles of pine kindlings, which was so written and spelled that the next day one hundred bundles of pine shingles were found encumbering the stairway of the warehouse, and when this blunder was traced home to Master John's handwriting, he was notified that the firm of Picul, Sapan, & Company had no further need for his services. Then his much-enduring uncles, by much letter-writing and vigilant attendance at many congressional district conventions, got him nominated by their member of Congress to a cadetship at West Point. This gentleman was called *their member* because they had *quoad hoc* bought him by such services. But when Master John presented himself for examination at West Point, he was so uncertain whether eleven times eleven were a hundred and seven, or whether it were not a hundred and seventeen, that he was passed by, and a little Irish boy, named Phil Sheridan, who had no uncles that were ever heard of, was taken in his place. How much the country lost in that substitution can never be told. After a similar experience as to a midshipman's berth, Master John had been left to follow up his own views in the training for a gentleman. Sometimes, in terrible pinch for pocket-money, he would shovel sidewalks for the neighbors. He was always ready, in summer, to burn a good deal of powder in shooting beach-birds; but he had attained the age of twenty without the knowledge of any handicraft, mystery, or profession except that of catching flounders from the wharves of the seaport village where he lived.

It was, therefore, as I have said, welcomed as a special providence, almost, that a benignant government at the demand of the uncles aforesaid, was able to give to Mr. John Sapp a desk in the War Department.

The duties of this post he was told, and he found, were such as would "explain themselves" to him. The first duty was to come in at nine, and the second was to leave at three. Mr. Sapp soon learned the second duty very well, and even assisted in arrangements by which, at noon every day, the in-door clock of the department was crowded forward ten minutes so as to make duty number two the easier. As for the first duty, he was never perfect. But, as he justly said, it made no sort of difference whether he were there early or late. The truth is, that it was an economy to him to come late; because he then needed fewer cigars to go through the morning. After he did arrive, he had the "National Intelligencer" to read, and the "Madisonian," and the "Globe"; he had such letters to acknowledge as had been sent down open to his room; and he had to get rid of the time till three o'clock, as amended, came.

All this was very comfortable for many years, while it lasted. It might have lasted till now, but for a little accident. It happened, one day, that a woman with a black veil came into the room where Mr. Sapp was reading, with his feet on the mantelpiece, and handed him a letter. "Take a seat," said he; "I am engaged just now." So the widow took a seat, while Mr. Sapp finished an account of a prize fight in the "Madisonian." He then left her, and went upstairs to settle his bets on this fight with one of the gentlemen there; and the widow waited an hour. Then he came back; and she asked him if he would look at her letter. He looked at it, and told her she had come to the wrong office, and wrote a memorandum, which directed her to go to the head-quarters of the army. The poor woman said she had been there, and they had sent her to him. By this continued importunity she wearied Mr. Sapp; and he said, with some warmth, that he would be damned if he would be bullied by her or by anybody; that he knew his business, if at the head-quarters they did not know theirs, and that she had better leave the office, and that very quickly, too. And so Mr. Sapp relapsed to his cigar.

Now it happened that this lady was the widow of a major-general, and the sister of another who was acting as assistant-adjutant on the general staff. She was attending to a mere piece of detail, drawing the money due to her son, who had died in service. It was merely for her own convenience that she had stopped at the department herself; and, in an hour more, she had reported at head-quarters, as bidden by Mr. Sapp.

In twenty-four hours more, therefore, Mr. John Sapp had his arrears of pay paid up to him, was dismissed from the service of the government, and Mr. Dick Nave was appointed to the vacant desk. This gentleman was the next on the list; that was the reason he was appointed.

Mr. John Sapp was free of the world.

But, from that moment, Mr. Sapp had found his profession. He was, as you have seen from what he did and said to the widow, what is called a "civil servant." He had seen the color of Uncle Sam's money. It was paid in coin in those days: and Mr. Sapp knew how regular were the quarter days, and how bright the quarters and the halves. If he were prejudiced before against the meaner professions, in which one receives his pay from his fellow-men, how much more was he prejudiced against them now, when he had learned how well Uncle Sam pays, even if he pays but little, and how easy it had been for him, till this misfortune came, to do even less than he was paid for. A civil servant had Mr. John Sapp begun in life; and a civil servant he would remain.

So he returned home. But he did not return before two or three "own correspondents" had announced in the "Buncombe True Eagle" and the "Bobadil True Flag" that our distinguished fellow-citizen, Mr. John Sapp, having pressed a series of reforms in the War Department which cut off the perquisites of some of the epaulette wearers who were parading on Pennsylvania Avenue, had been hunted down by them with relentless hostility, and at last had been driven from the post which he had so bravely maintained. The "Eagle" intimated that the least sop thrown to these hungry beagles by Mr. Sapp would have silenced their howl. But he was not the man to bribe. He preferred to go down with his colors flying, although the yellow flag of corruption should be flaunted in the hot sirocco of political and party tergiversation; and, with this talisman of integrity wrapped about his form, he would present himself in his native town for the verdict of the people whose rights he had maintained. In this cloud of mixed metaphor, Mr. Sapp returned to Shirk Corners, and took up his quarters at the village hotel.

On consultation with his friends, Mr. Sapp offered himself as candidate for the legislature,—the great mistake of his life, as he afterwards declared. Uncle Sam, he said, required little, if he paid little; paid well what he paid; and, if a man's politics were right, asked no questions. But when a man offered himself for the legislature, there were a thousand questions; "and a feller did not understand; and then what could a feller do?" But this was after he had learned what was what. While he was learning, his friends advised him to be seen freely among the people, and to attach the young men to him, and to gain the respect of the solid men. So Mr. Sapp became a fine member of the Light Infantry, and paid the entrance fees. He joined the Silver Fountain Division of Sons of Temperance, and attended their meetings. He invited all gentlemen of respectability into the private office of the Shirk House, and treated to champagne and cigars. He took a half pew in the Methodist Church, and generally attended the occasional and evening services at the Church of the Disciples. He looked in at the editorial office of the "Spy" in the morning; and if he got a good letter from Washington in the afternoon, he sent it to the editor of the "Informer." He joined the reading-club, and made himself agreeable to the ladies. He subscribed to the Orphans' Home, so that he might win the suffrages of orphans. He held yarn for those who knit at the ladies' sewing society, and spun yarns for those who would listen. He was faithful in his attendance at primary meetings. He sat through the speaking of the boys at the quarterly school exhibitions. He permitted himself to be made a director of the Horse-Thief Association, and when there was a fire, he worked at the brakes of the engines till he was spelled. These little occupations I mention only by way of illustration. He said himself that this set of duties was endless, and that anybody who knew what hard work a feller had before he could go to the legislature, would never envy any man his seat. "For his part, he was sure that a civil servant did more mean work than any nigger of them all."

If he is to be the standard, I am sure I agree with him.

At last the time for nomination came, and Mr. Sapp was nominated by the old Whig line, which was then in the majority in Buncombe County. Had the

Democrats been in the majority, Mr. Sapp would have solicited their nomination. "It's best to be on the winning side," he said. In times of long peace, the army and the navy are generally unpopular; and the impression that Mr. Sapp had been snubbed by shoulder-strapped men was enough to bring him into favor. "We shall walk over the track," said Mr. Hopkirk, his principal backer; and Mr. Facer, though not so confident, offered three to one in betting on him.

But alas! the Democrats named a candidate; and some thorny come-outers named another: so there was no walking over the track. And, by the same ill luck which made our civil servant insult Mrs. Gen. Armitage, he happened to ask Deacon Whitman, the Most Grand Worthy of the Sons of Temperance, to step into his room on a cold day and try some hot punch he had been brewing. Who could ever have thought that a jolly-looking old cove like that was a deacon? The deacon published this invitation in the next "Water-Bucket." He added some comments, which drew forth some dozen lies from Mr. Hopkirk the next day in the "Spy." "The deacon's letter lost us all the temperance vote; and Mr. Hopkirk's lost us all the liberal vote,"—so was the vote of the liquor houses and their coteries called. Then one day, at a conference meeting, Brother Sapp was asked pointedly if he believed in the objectivity of the atonement. "How is a feller to know?" he said afterwards to Mr. Facer. And poor Mr. Sapp, not knowing, told the truth, and said that under certain circumstances he did, and other circumstances he did not. He said this in such a way as to offend the class-leader, who was a man of courage, and in the habit of saying yes for yes, and no for no. After a dozen other such pieces of ill-luck as this, it is no wonder that John Throop, the Independent, stood at the head of the poll; Reuben Gerry, the Democrat, came next, and John Sapp last of all. But he had all the liquor bills of his friends, all the printing of the canvass, and half of the bets upon it to pay.

By this time, John was thrown back upon his uncles again. As for them, worthy men, they had written so many letters of introduction in his favor that they began to believe their own words, and regarded him as a much abused man, and themselves as worse abused than he.

The earliest form of this letter which I have found is simply this:—

DEAR SIR,—I take the liberty to introduce to you my nephew, Mr. John Sapp, who will explain to you the object with which he calls. Respectfully yours,

PHILEMON PLAICE,
or AILANTHUS PLAICE, *as the case might be.*

But after the uncles became indignant themselves with the public's dulness, and especially after they found they were paying John Sapp's bills, the letters became eloquent enlargements on these themes.

MY DEAR FRIEND,—The bearer, my nephew, Mr. John Sapp, is a young gentleman who has been very hardly treated in the public service. He calls to ask your advice and interest in an application he is making for—

For whatever it might happen to be; as, the post of superintendent of oil lamps;

Of chief marshal of the Kossuth procession;
Of county surveyor (duties done by proxy);
Of assistant marshal for the census;
Of assistant assessor;
Of pilot commissioner;
Of librarian of the Archæological Institute;
Of messenger in the State House;
Of head of the lamplighting bureau in the City Hall;
Of ticket-seller at the Coliseum;
Of lecturer for the Free Trade League;
Of trustee of the Protectionist Fund;
Of secretary to the Board of Health;
Of auditor of the Alabama claims;
Of secretary to the commissioners at Vienna;
Of clerk to the inspectors of Ward 2;

Or whatever other function might prove to need a functionary. Indeed, the Messrs. Plaice soon persuaded themselves that he had special fitness, in turn, for any and all posts which fell vacant:—

For inspector of fish, because his father went on a mackerel voyage when he was a boy.

For toll-keeper of the Potomac bridge, because his mother was of a misanthropic turn of mind.

For firewarden, because he was blown up with gunpowder when he was a child. And with each rebuff in Mr. John Sapp's line of applications, his uncles were the more indignant for the ingratitude of the world.

So was Mr. Sapp; but none the less did he push his traverses towards the works of what he called the common enemy.

He was at one time urging his claims to be employed inspector of Orange Peel, as it was found on sidewalks,—a post for which he was specially fitted, because a boy with whom he went to school was our consul at Fayal. Some one who met him said, very unkindly, that John Sapp's life seemed to be a very easy one; and the phrase came to John's ears. "Easy?" said he. "I should like to know what is hard. This fellow thinks all you have to do is to ask to be appointed Inspector of Orange Peel, and then to begin to draw the salary. Shows what he knows of our business.

"Now see; this inspector is appointed by the county commissioners. Have to find out who they are. Make no mistake. Get the names right first,—all the letters right. William Claflin and Tennie Claflin's husband not the same man, —very different men. Then find out their friends,—where they go to church, who's the minister, who's the doctor, what bank they're in, and so on. Then find out who knows the friends. See?

"Then begin. Speak first to John Jones at the barber's or post-office quite accidentally. Get John Jones to give you letter—see?—to introduce you to David Dodder. See? Simple letter,—general letter. 'Friend Mr. Sapp,—little matter of business.' Then call on David Dodder—see?—after dinner, when he's good-natured. Ask him to introduce you to William Belcher,—'important matter of business, necessary for public benefit.' See? Then go to William Belcher,—best coat on, clean shirt, shaved on purpose,—and ask him for letter of introduction to county commissioners,—knows 'em all,—see?— something like this:—

"'My dear Mr. Sheriff,—Will you present to the county commissioners my friend Mr. John Sapp, who is a candidate for the Inspection of Orange Peel? I do not personally know Mr. Sapp, whose public service has been mostly at Washington; but my friend, Mr. Dodder, on whose judgment I rely, &c., &c. See?

"Now," said Mr. Sapp, when he explained this, "what man says it is easy to get those letters together? What man says I did not earn this inspectorship by hard work? And when a fellow's got it, I'll be hanged if the Know-nothings did not come in before I had been in office a week, and before I had any chance to join them; and I was turned out before I had inspected one orange!"

Mr. Carlyle says that the hatter of the present day, instead of exerting himself to make good hats, exerts himself to write good advertisements of hats, or to make the largest hat that can be made of lath and plaster, to be carted round the streets of London upon wheels, bearing advertisements of his hat store. The evil is not a new one. The cat in Æsop told the fox that she had but one way to save her life, if the enemy should come. "How sad!" said the fox. "I have a hundred; and I will explain them to you." Just as he began to explain, the hounds dashed upon them. The cat ran up a tree, and was safe; but the fox, at the end of his hundredth turn, was devoured. Mr. John Sapp was as badly off as the fox. He was fit for a hundred places, but he never could stay in one of them. Had he known how to do one thing, he could have done it his life long.

For, when a crisis comes, or anything like a crisis, the world has a hopeless fashion of jamming its old stout felt hat over its ears, tying a stout scarf above it, and going out to battle in the storm, and forgets, in the fight, the lath-and-plaster hat which has dragged the street yesterday. It trusts a proved friend, though his felt be a little rough, and his braid a little frayed. And while Mr. John Sapp's portfolio of recommendations grew larger and larger, and showed he was good for everything, from a post on the Board of Health round to the janitorship of the public library, the public, when it was on its mettle, had a brutal way of appointing what he called "new men," who had made no application, or what he called "old fogies," who had been trained by experience to understand their duties. And it must be confessed that Mr. Sapp held back very modestly from the places which involved danger to-day, or which required preparation in years bygone. When the war came, he made no offer of service in the field, but was quite sure there must be some place as storekeeper that he should like. When Kansas was to be settled of a sudden, he did not think of emigrating; but he thought there might be some place for him in the office that sent the emigrants. I happen to remember that forty-nine thousand, nine hundred and ninety-nine other men of his age thought much the same thing. Having, indeed, been educated for nothing in particular, Mr. Sapp was always on the front list of applicants for places where there was nothing in particular to do.

I have had a great many such men to examine, sooner or later. If Mr. Sapp had come before me, sitting as county commissioner, or inspector of prisons, the question I would have put him first would have been, "What can you do best in this world? What do you think you are most good for? What do you like to do?" It is pathetic to see how disappointed men break down under that question. I once asked a foreign missionary what he would do if he had *carte-blanche*,—had a hundred thousand dollars to expend in the next year?

"I—I—I think, ah, ah—you had better ask the advisory board," he said.

There was nothing in particular that he wanted to do; and so he did nothing. I used to ask young men what they were reading, but I do not now, unless I am quite sure of them. So many men said, "Oh,—really, you know,—the newspapers, you know,—and the magazines, you know,—'Littell's' and 'Old and New' and the 'Atlantic,' you know—must keep up with the times, you know." I did not know any such thing. They read nothing in particular, and practically read nothing at all. Now, the people,—who are, on the whole, wiser than we think,—when their moments of crisis come, sweep all such

Jacks-of-all-trades by. They light on some one man, who has done some one thing well. He has made fish leap up the falls at Lowell into the Merrimack. He has taught the waves to obey his bidding, and sheer off the shore at Chicago. He has administered a railroad, so that no widow weeps when she hears its name, no orphan curses the recklessness of its managers. The grateful people know such men. And when a crisis comes, that voice of the people, which is as the voice of God, says to such a man,—

"Thou hast been faithful in a few things: I will make thee ruler over many things. Thou hast been faithful in a very little. Have thou authority over ten cities!"

But Mr. Sapp heard no such order to come up higher. The truth is, that, in three cases out of four, official life with us is not a good training for business in any other work. And Mr. Sapp's office at the War Department had been one of those three cases. It had taught him to file letters, to note their contents in an alphabetical index, to refer them respectfully to somebody else, to write back in an invariable form to the authors that they had been respectfully referred, and, once a week, to send a volume of letters to the binder. But this was all that it taught him. The consequence was that when he was appointed to any function with any different duties, he functioned ill.

Thus he was a poor librarian at the Archæological; and the directors voted not to have any librarian. They appointed a superintendent; and Mr. Sapp was discharged.

He lectured ill for the Free Trade League, so that the people stayed at home. Now, as Lord Dundreary says, "How can a feller lecture, if people will not listen?"

He inspected orange peel ill, so that, whether the Know-nothings had come in or not, he would have gone out. In truth, he was, as I said, trained to do nothing in particular; and the only place he was fit for, therefore, was some place where there was nothing in particular to do.

In the English civil service there are many such places; but in that of America there are very few.

The last time I saw Mr. Sapp, he was standing rather ruefully at the door of Dr. Chloral's office. Dr. Chloral, you remember, is the celebrated dentist of that name, with the striking sign on Cambridge Street, where a gutta-perch mouth, propelled by Cochituate, opens and shuts to slow music, as if it were listening to a lyceum lecture two-thirds done. Fortunately for me, Mr. Sapp did not see me.

At that moment he was laying his lines for an inspectorship in the Custom

House. He had no letter of introduction which he thought would move Judge Russell, the collector. But he knew, or thought he knew, that Dr. Chloral and Judge Russell were intimate; so he stood at Dr. Chloral's street-door till some patient might come in whom Mr. Sapp could engage to introduce him to the dentist, who in his turn could then introduce him to the collector.

An admirable plan! Well, many patients came, you may be sure. Ladies came in carriages with their children, from Chester Square. Students came in the Union cars from Cambridge. Laboring men came up from North Street. Later in the day, toothaching bankers came from State Street, and neuralgic aldermen from City Hall. But hour passed after hour; and no man came whom Mr. Sapp could ask for an introduction to Dr. Chloral. Hour passed after hour. The clock struck three, when Mr. Sapp knew that office hours were over for that day. The hard-worked doctor, released at last, came running down to take his walk before dinner, when lo, one more patient on the stairway!

It was poor John Sapp. Failing other introduction, he had, with the promptness of genius, invented a toothache.

He met Dr. Chloral, and acted agony so well, that he compelled the doctor to return.

"But there's nothing the matter with that tooth, man! It is sound for thirty years."

"O," said Mr. Sapp, "I wish I thought so!"

"Why, man, I wish it were in my head!" said the doctor.

"O," said Mr. Sapp, "I wish it were!"

"Well," said Dr. Chloral, "if you say so, here goes"; and in a moment he pulled as honest a tooth as ever ground gristle or tendon.

"Now rinse your mouth here, sir; here's a towel, sir; I'm rather late, sir"; and then, as Mr. Sapp loitered,—

"What else can I do for you?"

"Could not you,—Dr. Chloral,—could not you write me a line of introduction to Mr. Collector Russell at the Custom House?"

"And after all, do you think," said Mr. Sapp,—"after all, Judge Russell appointed a one-legged soldier, who had served in the war; and I lost my tooth for nothing."

After this repulse, Mr. Sapp became low in his mind. His uncles were dead,— that is, his real uncles were; and he carried to his other uncles most of his portable property for pawn. At last he got up a paper which many men signed

—without reading it. They hoped, perhaps, it was a petition to the governor that he would give Mr. Sapp a place, holding for good behavior, in the state-prison. It *was* a recommendation to the benevolent to subscribe for his relief. With this paper he called, as it happened, on Mrs. Gen. Armitage, who was spending the summer at the sea-shore at Shirk Corners. Mrs. Armitage was interested in the fate of the worn-out office-seeker. She gave him a chair, a piece of cake, and a glass of water, and made him tell his whole story. To her dismay, she found that *she* had been the arbiter of his fortunes. She had long since forgotten his rudeness, and he had never known her name. But Mrs. Armitage gave him five dollars; and, thinking that she had, perhaps, some influence still in Washington, wrote a confidential note to a very, very, very high authority, to know if there was really no place, with ever so little salary, —in which a man could just live,—which Mr. Sapp could have. "Some place, you know," said she, "where there is nothing in particular to do, but where you just want a single man, who does not drink, and who, I believe, does not steal."

The answer, alas! was—as it always is—that nothing was vacant but the consulate at Fernando Po. The quarter's fees there were never more than fifty-seven dollars. How much they would be in a year, no one knows; for no consul has ever survived that climate more than four months. But it is thought that the fees may be larger now; for no one has applied for the place since the last consul died, seven years ago. This is the only place in the gift of the government that no one has applied for.

Mrs. Armitage showed this letter to Mr. John Sapp. "Have you ever lived in a warm climate?" said she kindly. "There can be no danger of rheumatism there."

No, there could be no danger of rheumatism; but, for all that, Mr. Sapp declined the offer. It did him good to decline it. He wrote a letter on square letter-paper, and sealed it with his father's seal-ring. It was the first thing in life he had ever declined!

I think that seal touched them in Washington. They are hard-hearted, but sealing-wax—real red sealing-wax—touches them when rhetoric is powerless.

I think so. For the next week came this letter, autograph from the very, very, very high authority:—

WASHINGTON, April 1, 18—

DEAR MRS. ARMITAGE,—We must send at once, without noise, a trusty man to take possession of the Island of St. Lazarus, one of Aleutian group, west of Alaska, in the name of the United States. It will be some years before we establish a post there; but meanwhile the flag must be kept flying.

Would your friend like this? There is a sealer's hut there; and he will have his passage free, full rations, and stationery. I think he also has the franking privilege for all official correspondence. I will inquire at the post-office. He will be commissioned as Governor-General of the island; but there are no inhabitants except the seals, unless he chooses to take his family with him.

This was a long letter for the very high authority. "He forgets," said Mrs. Armitage, "that I told him that Mr. Sapp was a single man!" And from that time she bore that grudge against the very high authority which a woman always bears against a man who does not read her letters twice through.

Mr. Sapp was delighted. He had been appointed confidentially to an office for which he had never applied. It was a secret office. No man knew of it. He accepted the appointment, for no bondsmen were required. He was distressed to find that no oath was to be taken. He went to Washington to receive his instructions, which was quite unnecessary. He drew on the navy yard at Charlestown for stationery, and he drew for a great deal. There was one large tin box filled with red tape, which was his especial glory.

He was landed at St. Lazarus prosperously; and, with the assistance of a boat's crew, they got the flag flying. They cleared out the sealer's house. They carried up ten barrels of salt junk, twelve of salt pork, thirteen of potatoes, fourteen of flour, fifteen of sour-krout, and sixteen of white beans. These were the supplies Mr. John Sapp was to subsist on for a year. They carried up four reams of foolscap paper, ruled and margined, for his official reports to the War Department; four of quarto letter-paper, for his reports to the Navy; four of royal octavo, for his reports to the Smithsonian; four of large congress note, for his reports to the Weather Bureau; four of small congress note, for his reports to the Treasury; and four of gilt-edged note, with initials J. S., for his private correspondence. They carried up eleven pounds of red sealing-wax, the tin box of red tape they carried up; and so they bade him good-by. The boat returned to the ship. Then it proved that his dog and cat and parrot and umbrella were still on board; and the captain's gig was sent with them. So Mr. Sapp was not left alone.

Here was a *place*. It was a place with nothing particular to do; and Mr. Sapp was left to do it.

He kept no diary. Nothing, therefore, is known of his experience for the year, but when, the next year, the store-ship landed his stores, the boatswain in charge ran up the beach, and met a grave man in seal-skins, who made a military salute.

The boatswain saluted him, and was about to speak, when old Sealskin, as he afterwards called him, said, "Have you passed quarantine!"

"Quarantine? No, sir!"

"Take your boat round into the South Cove, and see the health officer, and bring me his permit."

The boatswain, from habit of obedience, obeyed,—took the boat round in half an hour's pulling. Health officer! There were some stupid seals who jumped off the rocks; and that was all.

The captain of the store-ship, meanwhile, had seen this manoeuvre with amazement, and sent a second boat ashore. With this boat, he sent his second officer. He also met the lonely Robinson, and saluted.

"Have you passed quarantine?"

"All right, my man," said the friendly sailor; and Sealskin turned, and walked with him to his hut. A moment more, and the boatswain followed. He could find no health officer, he said.

"It must be past his office hours," said Mr. Sapp gravely. "They close at eleven there. You shall be examined to-morrow."

The boatswain stared at this postponement of quarantine; but then, on a word from his superior officer, he produced a bag of papers and letters for Mr. Sapp, which he had been afraid to offer him before.

"They will be respectfully fumigated and respectfully referred," said Mr. Sapp.

And he hung them to the crane in the chimney.

Then he lifted off a pot of bean-soup, and filled a bowl for each of the wondering men. He produced hard-tack from a closet, and whiskey and water. And then, still asking no question, he took down the smoky letters, and opened them slowly.

But, to the men's amazement, he did not read one.

He folded the first with a steel letter file, two inches and a quarter wide, and docketed it,—"Received June 11. Respectfully referred to Next Friday, Esq., P.M."

When the boatswain heard of Mr. Friday, he thought it was surely Robinson Crusoe.

But the next letter, unread, was filed and docketed—"Respectfully referred to Next Saturday, Esq., A.M."

"P.M. and A.M.," cried the boatswain; "they have masters of arts here as well as postmasters."

"Not at all," said the governor severely; "A.M.—Ante-Meridiem; P.M.,—

Post-Meridiem"; and without reading the next letter, he filed it, and indorsed it,—"Respectfully referred to Next Sunday, Esq., M."

"Young man," said he, "I shall examine and file this letter on Friday afternoon; this one on Saturday morning; this on Sunday noon. Let all things be done regularly and in order."

The mate and boatswain were alarmed. They hastily finished their bean-soup and fled to the boat, returning with six men, who rolled a barrel of junk up the well-kept gravel walk.

"Invoice?" said the governor.

There was no invoice.

"Prepare an invoice."

And the meek boatswain obeyed.

"My man, take this to the inspector," said Mr. Sapp to one of the crew, after he had indorsed it,—"Respectfully referred to the Inspector-General."

The sailor was a Portuguese,—understood no English; bobbed his head, and waited for light.

Mr. Sapp led him to the door, and pointed to a bearded walrus,—who sat on a rock above the landing,—bidding him take the invoice to him, and land nothing more without his orders.

Poor man!—or happy man shall I call him? He had what he sought for. He had a place with nothing to do, and faithfully he had done it,—so faithfully that, in that sad loyalty, the little fragment of his untrained wits gave way.

NICOLETTE AND AUCASSIN.

A TROUBADOUR'S TALE.

[I have introduced the beginning of this romance in my little story called "In His Name." In the form in which the reader sees it, it belongs to the twelfth century, in which the action of that story is laid. The French critics think they have found traces of the narrative at a time even earlier. Some of the English critics have spoken of the story with more harshness than I think it deserves. Aucassin's bitter contrast of the hell and heaven of which he has been taught is certainly in character; and the reader must give no more weight to it than it deserves.]

I.

Who will listen yet again
To the old and jovial strain,—
The old tale of love that's always new?
  She's a girl that's fair as May;
  He's a boy as fresh as day;
And the story is as gay as it is true.

II.

Who will hear the pretty tale
Of my thrush and nightingale,—
Of the dangers and the sorrows that they met?
  How he fought without a fear,
  For his charming little dear,—
Aucassin and his loving Nicolette?

III.

For, my lords, I tell you true
That you never saw or knew,
Man or woman so ugly or so gray,
  Who would not all day long,
  Sit and listen to the song
And the story that I tell you here to-day.

Now you must know, my lords and my ladies, that the Count Bougars de Valence chose to make war with the Count Garin de Beaucaire. And the war was so cruel, that the count never let one day go by, but that he came thundering at the walls and barriers of the town, with a hundred knights, and with ten thousand men-at-arms, on foot and on horseback, who burned all the houses, and stole all the sheep, and killed all the people that they could.

Now the Count Garin de Beaucaire was very old, and was sadly broken with years. He had used his time very ill, had the Count de Beaucaire. And the old wretch had no heir, either son or daughter, except one boy, whose name was

AUCASSIN.

Aucassin was gentle and handsome. He was tall and well made. His legs were good, and his feet were good; his body was good, and his arms were good. His hair was blonde, a little curly. His eyes were like gray fur, for they were near silver, and near blue, and they laughed when you looked at them. His nose was high and well placed. His face was clear and winning. Yes, and he had everything charming, and nothing bad about him. But this young man was so wholly conquered by love (who conquers everybody), that he would not occupy himself in any other thing. He would not be a knight; he would not take arms; he would not go to the tourneys; he would not do any of the things he ought to do.

His father was very much troubled by this, and he said to him one morning,—

"My son, take your arms, mount your horse, defend your country, protect your people. If they only see you in the midst of them, this will give them more courage; they will fight all the better for their lives and their homes, for your land and mine."

"Father," said Aucassin, "why do you say this to me?

"May God never hear my prayers, if I ever mount horse, or go to tourney or to battle, before you have yourself given to me my darling Nicolette,—my sweetheart whom I love so dearly."

"My son," said the father to him, "this cannot be.

"Give up forever your dreams of this captive girl, whom the Saracens brought from some strange land, and sold to the viscount here.

"He trained her; he baptized her; she is his god-child.

"Some day he will give her to some brave fellow who will have to gain his bread by his sword.

"But you, my son, when the time comes that you wish to take a wife, I will give you some king's daughter, or at least the daughter of a count.

"There is not in all France a man so rich that you may not marry his daughter, if you choose."

So said the old man. But Aucassin replied,—

"Alas, my father! there is not in this world the principality which would not be honored, if my darling Nicolette, my sweetest, went to live there.

"If she were queen of France or of England, if she were empress of Germany or of Constantinople, she could not be more courteous or more gracious; she could not have sweeter ways or greater virtues."

[*Now they sing it.*]
　　All the night and all the day
　　Aucassin would beg and pray,—
"Oh, my father! give my Nicolette to me."
　　Then his mother came to say,—
"What is it that my foolish boy can see?"

　　"Nicolette is sweet and gay."

　　"But Nicolette's a slave.—
　　If a wife my boy would have,

Let him choose a lady fair of high degree."
  "Oh, no! my mother, no!
  For I love my darling so!
  Her face is always bright,
  And her footstep's always light;
  And I cannot let my dainty darling go.
No, mother dear, she rules my heart;
No, mother dear, we cannot part."

[Now they speak it, and talk it, and tell it.]

When the Count Garin de Beaucaire saw that he could not drag Nicolette out from the heart of Aucassin, he went to find the viscount, who was his vassal; and he said to him,—

"Sir Viscount, we must get rid of your god-child Nicolette.

"Cursed be the country where she was born! for she is the reason why I am losing my Aucassin, who ought to be a knight, and who refuses to do what he ought to do.

"If I can catch her, I will burn her at the stake, and I will burn you too."

"My lord," replied the viscount, "I am very sorry for what has happened; but it is no fault of mine.

"I bought Nicolette with my money; I trained her; I had her baptized; and she is my god-child.

"I wanted to marry her to a fine young man of mine, who would gladly have earned her bread for her, which is more than your son Aucassin could do.

"But, since your wish and your pleasure are what they are, I will send this god-child of mine away to such a land, in such a country, that Aucassin shall never set his eyes upon her again."

"See that you do so!" cried the Count Garin to the viscount, "or great misfortunes will come to you."

So saying, he left his vassal.

Now the viscount had a noble palace, of high walls, surrounded by a thickly planted garden. He put Nicolette into one of the rooms of this palace, in the very highest story.

She had an old woman for her only companion, with enough bread and meat and wine, and everything else that they needed to keep them alive.

Then he fastened and concealed the door, so that no one could go in; and he left no other opening but the window, which was very narrow, and opened on the garden.

Nicolette was put in prison;
  And a vaulted room
Wonderfully built and painted
  Was her prison home.

The pretty maiden came
To the marble window-frame:
  Her hair was light,
  Her eyes were bright,
And her face was a charming face to see.
  No; never had a knight a maid
With such a charming face to see.

  She looked into the garden close,
  And there she saw the open rose,
  Heard the thrushes sing and twitter,—
  And she sang in accent bitter,—
  "Oh! why am I a captive here?
  Why locked up in cruel walls?
Aucassin, my sweetheart dear,
  Whom my heart its master calls,
I have been your sweetheart for this livelong year:
  That is why I've come
  To this vaulted room;
But by God, the son of Mary, no!
I will not be captured so,
If only I can break away, and go."

[Now they speak it, and talk it, and tell it.]

So Nicolette was put in prison, as you have just heard; and soon a cry and noise ran through the country that she was lost. Some said that she had run away; others said that the Count Garin de Beaucaire had killed her.

All in despair at the joy which this news seemed to cause to some people, Aucassin went to find the viscount of the town.

"Lord Viscount," he asked him, "what have you done with Nicolette, my sweetest love, the thing in all the world which I love best?

"You have stolen her!

"Be sure, Viscount, that, if I die of this, the blame shall fall on you.

"For surely it is you who tear away my life in tearing away my darling Nicolette!"

"Fair sir," answered the viscount, "do let this Nicolette alone, for she is not worthy of you. She is a slave whom I have bought with my *deniers;* and she must serve as a wife to a young fellow of her own state, to a poor man, and not to a lord like you, who ought to marry none but a king's daughter, or at least a count's daughter.

"What should you be doing for yourself, if you did make a lady of this vile creature, and marry her?

"Then would you be very happy indeed, very happy; for your soul would abide forever in hell, and never should you enter into paradise."

"Into paradise?" repeated Aucassin angrily. "And what have I to do there? I do not care to go there if it be not with Nicolette, my sweetest darling whom I love so much.

"Into paradise? And do you know who those are that go there,—you who think it is a place where I must wish to go? They are old priests, old cripples, old one-eyed men, who lie day and night before the altars, sickly, miserable, shivering, half-naked, half-fed, dead already before they die. These are they who go to paradise; and they are such pitiful companions, that I do not desire to go to paradise with them.

"But to hell would I gladly go; for to hell go the good clerks, and the fair knights slain in battle and in great wars, the brave sergeants-at-arms, and the men of noble lineage; and with all these would I gladly go."

"Stop!" says the viscount. "All which you can say, and nothing at all, are exactly the same thing. Never shall you see Nicolette again.

"What you and I may get for this would not be pleasant, if you still will be complaining.

"We all might be burned by your father's command,—Nicolette, you, and I myself into the bargain."

"Despair!" said Aucassin to himself. And he left the viscount, who was quite as much disturbed as he.

[*Now they sing it.*]

Then Aucassin went home;
But his heart was wrung with fear
By the parting from his dainty dear,
  His dainty dear so fair,
  Whom he sought for everywhere;
But nowhere could he find her, far or near.

To his palace he has come,
  And he climbs up every stair:
He hides him in his room,
  And weeps in his despair.

  "Oh, my Nicolette!" said he,
"So dear and sweet is she!
  So sweet for that, so sweet for this,
  So sweet to speak, so sweet to kiss,
So sweet to come, so sweet to stay,

So sweet to sing, so sweet to play,
  So sweet when there, so sweet when here,
  Oh, my darling! Oh, my dear!
  Where are you, my sweet, while I
  Sit and weep so near to die,
Because I cannot find my darling dear?"[1]

[Now they speak it, and talk it, and tell it.]

[1] The original is very pretty, and can be guessed out, even by the unlearned reader:—

"Nicolete biax esters,
Biax venir et biax alers
Biax déduis et dous parlers,
Biax borders et biax jouers,
Biax baisiers, biax acolers."

  Biax is *beata.*

Now, while Aucassin was mourning thus in his room, always grieving for Nicolette his love, the Count Bougars de Valence was keeping up his war against the Count Garin de Beaucaire.

He had drawn out his footmen and his horsemen to assault the castle; and the defendants of the castle seized their arms to meet him, and ran to the gates and walls where they thought the besiegers would attack. The people of the town followed the knights and the sergeants: they mounted the ramparts, and poured down a storm of quarrels and javelins.

In the very most terrible moment of the assault, the Count Garin de Beaucaire came into the room where Aucassin was grieving in his sorrow for his sweet darling, Nicolette.

"Oh, my boy!" he said, "what are you doing here while your castle is besieged, good and strong though it be? Do you know, that, if you lose it, you are disinherited? Boy, take your arms, mount your horse, defend your lands, and lead your men to battle. As soon as they see you in the midst of them, they will bravely defend their homes and their lives, your lands and mine. You are tall and strong; and you ought to show that you are."

"Father," replied Aucassin, "what are you talking about? May God refuse me all that I may ever ask him, if I consent to be made a knight, to mount a horse, or to go to fight, before you have given me Nicolette, my darling sweetheart!"

"Boy," replied his father, "this cannot be. I had rather be disinherited, and lose all I have, than that you should have her for your wife."

On this the Count Garin de Beaucaire turned away. But Aucassin called him back, and said to him, "Come, father, I beg you! I have one condition to propose to you."

"What is that, dear boy?"

"It is this. I will take my arms, I will mount my horse, and I will do my duty bravely, on condition that, if God bring me out of the battle unhurt, you will let me see my darling sweetheart, Nicolette, and embrace her. There shall be time to say two or three words to her, and to kiss her once."

"I grant it willingly," said the father; and he went away.

[Now they sing it.]

Not diamonds bright, or heaps of gold
    Would give to you such bliss
As blessed this boy when he was told
    The way to earn a kiss.

They quickly brought him arms of steel,
    His helmet and his crest;
Upon his head the helmet laced;
And then a double hauberk braced
    Across his breast.

He springs upon his charger white;
And when he glances on his feet
His greaves are tight and silver bright:
His darling dear he thinks upon;
He spurs his war-horse fleet,
And rushes straight before him down
      To the fight.

[Here they speak it, and talk it, and tell it.]

Aucassin was armed, then, as you have heard.

How bright his shield, as it hung from his neck! how well his helmet fitted his head! and how his sword clanged, hanging upon his thigh!

The young man was tall, strong, handsome, and well armed. His horse was swift; and he was soon at the castle-gate.

Now, do not go and think that he was thinking the least in the world of capturing oxen or cows or goats! No, nor of giving mortal blows to the knights or the other soldiers of Count Bougars de Valence!

Oh, no, not he! He had something else in his head and in his heart; for he was thinking of Nicolette, his darling sweetheart. So he even forgot to hold up his reins; and his horse, as soon as he once felt the spurs, carried him in full *mêlée* into the very middle of his enemies.

They were overjoyed at such luck. They surrounded him, and seized his lance and his shield, and, as they led him away prisoner, began to ask each other with what death they would make him die.

"Alas!" said Aucassin to himself, "these are my mortal enemies, who are leading me away to cut off my head. But, if my head is cut off, I shall never be able to speak again to Nicolette, my darling sweetheart."

Then he added, "I still have my good sword. I am mounted on a strong horse. If he does not save me from the *mêlée*, it is because he never loved me, and then may God never help him!"

So he grasped his sword in his hand, and drove his spurs into his horse's side again, and struck to right, and struck to left, and cut and thrust. At every blow, he chopped off heads and arms, and all around him he made the place bloody and empty, as a boar does when he is assailed by dogs in a forest. Ten knights were thus maimed, and seven others were wounded. Then he withdrew at once from the *mêlée* with his horse at full gallop, still grasping his sword in his hand.

Now the Count Bougars de Valence had heard they had captured his enemy Aucassin, and that they were going to hang him. He came up there at just this moment. Aucassin recognized him, and struck him a heavy blow with his sword full on his helmet, so that it was crushed down upon his head, and he fell stunned upon the ground. Then the young man took him by the hand to help him up, and, as soon as he could stand, took him by the nose-piece of his helmet, and led him, without more ado, to his father, the Count Garin de Beaucaire, to whom he said,—

"Father, here is your enemy, who has fought so long against you, and done you so much mischief. This war which he has made against you has lasted now for twenty years, and no one has been able to bring it to a good end. But I hope it is finished to-day."

"Dear son," replied the old count, "such feats of youth as this are worth much more than your foolish loves."

"Father," replied Aucassin, "do not begin to preach to me, I beg you. Think, rather, of keeping the promise which you gave to me."

"What promise, my dear boy?"

"What! have you already forgotten it, my father? By my head! forget it who will, I shall remember it. What! my father, do you not remember, that when I consented to arm myself, and go and fight this count's people, it was on condition that, if God should bring me out of the battle unhurt, you would let me see my darling sweetheart, Nicolette, and say two or three words to her, and kiss her once? As you promised this, my father, so you must perform."

"I hear," replied the count; "but I do not understand. It is impossible that I ever promised anything so foolish. Why, if your Nicolette was here, I should burn her without pity, and you yourself might expect the same fate."

"Is that all, my father?" said Aucassin.

"Yes," replied the count.

"*Certes*" replied the boy, "I am very sorry to see a man of your age such a liar!"

Then he turned towards the Count de Valence, and said to him, "Count de Valence, are you not my prisoner?"

"Certainly."

"Give me your hand, then, I beg you."

"Gladly," replied the count; and he placed his hand in Aucassin's.

Aucassin replied, "Count de Valence, pledge me your faith that, whenever you have the wish or the power to shame my father, or to hurt him, in his person or in his goods, you will do so."

"*Pardieu*, sir! do not mock me, but name my ransom. Ask for gold or silver, horses or palfreys, dogs or birds, and I will try to give you what you ask. This is another thing."

"What!" cried Aucassin, "do you not own yourself my prisoner?"

"Indeed I do," cried the Count de Bougars.

"Well, if you will not take the oath I demand, your head shall fly off."

"Enough! I take the oath you exact," said the count quickly.

Then Aucassin ordered a horse for him, mounted another, and led him to a place of safety.

> [*Now they sing it.*]
> Now when the Count Garin
> Finds out that Aucassin
>   His darling sweet
>   Will not forget,
> His darling of the charming face,
>   He claps him in a dungeon,
>   In a cellar underground,
> All walled in with heavy stones,
>   Built double thick around;
>   And my wretched Aucassin
>   So sad as now had never been.
>
>   "Oh, my darling Nicolette!"
>   In his misery said he,

69

"My darling dear of charming face,
My darling *fleur de lis*,
My darling sweeter than the grape,
My darling, list to me,
Imprisoned in this horrid place.

"The other day a pilgrim gray
From Limousin had made his way,
And on the straw the poor man lay,
So sick was he, and near to die.
But Nicolette passed by his door.
The pilgrim heard my darling's feet
Pit-pat across the floor;
He saw my darling's little cloak
Her cape so white, her ermine bright;
And though no word she spoke,
Yet, when he saw my darling sweet,
The poor old pilgrim raised his head,
And, cured by her, he left his bed,
And took his staff, and took his way,
And found his home once more.

"Oh, darling dear! oh, *fleur de lis!*
So sweet to come, so sweet to stay,
So sweet to sing, so sweet to play,
So sweet for that, so sweet for this,
So sweet to speak, so sweet to kiss,
Who is there who my love can see,
And hate a girl so sweet as she?
For you, dear child, your love is bound
In this dungeon underground:
Here they will see me die alone
For you, my *fleur de lis!*"

[*Now they speak it, and talk it, and tell it.*]

Aucassin was thrown into prison, as you have just heard. And Nicolette, on her part, was still in the vaulted room, imprisoned also.

It was in the summer-time in the month of May, when the days are so warm, and so long, and so full of light, and the nights so sweet and so serene. Nicolette lay in her bed, and saw the moon shine clear through the window, and heard the nightingale sing among the trees of the garden. She remembered Aucassin, the friend she loved so well, and she began to sigh tenderly. Then she thought upon the deadly hatred of the Count Garin de Beaucaire, and she knew that she was lost if she remained in this room, and that her dear Aucassin would be lost also if he remained in his dungeon.

Then she looked at the old woman who was set to guard her, and she saw that she was asleep. Nicolette rose quickly, threw a fine silk mantle which she had saved over her shoulders, took the sheets and coverlet of her bed, made of them as long a rope as she could, and tied it to the window-post. When she had done this, she seized it with both hands, one above, and one below, and slid down upon the turf, which was covered with dew.

Thus she descended into the garden.

Nicolette's hair was blonde, fine, and curly; her eyes were soft and laughing; her complexion was fair and fresh; her nose high and well placed; her lips were redder than cherries and roses in summer-time, and her teeth white and small. You could span her little waist with your two hands; and the daisies which she broke when she stepped upon them, as they fell back upon her ankles, seemed black against her feet, so fair was this girl.

She went to the garden-gate and opened it; she walked through the streets of Beaucaire by the light of the moon, and strayed here, and strayed there, till she found the tower in which was her sweetheart, Aucassin. Now, this tower had loopholes in it on each side.

Nicolette crept in behind one of the pillars, and wrapped herself in her mantle, and thrust her blonde head into one of the crevices, so that she could hear the voice of her dear Aucassin, who was weeping within bitterly, in great grief for the loss of his darling sweetheart, who was absent from his eyes. And, when Nicolette had heard him, she resolved to speak to him, in turn.

> [*Now they sing it.*]
> Nicolette, of lovely face,
> Rested in this darksome place,
>   Against a pillar, where
> The heavy wall her lover kept:
> She heard her darling as he wept
>   In his despair.
>
> Then, in turn, to him she cried,
>   "Aucassin, of noble race,
>   Freeman born, and proud of place,
> Why should you complain and grieve,
> Because you must your sweetheart leave?
>   Your father fain would burn me,
>   And all your kinsmen spurn me.
> From you, my darling love, I flee:
> I shall go and cross the sea,
> In other lands than this to be."
>
> Then she cut off her golden hair,
> And threw it to her lover there.
>   Each heavy lock, each pretty curl,
>   Aucassin in rapture prest,
>   And hid them on his panting breast,
>   While he wept in his despair
>   For his darling girl.

[*Now they speak it, and talk it, and tell it.*]

Now, when Aucassin heard Nicolette say that she going to another country, he was very much distressed.

"My darling sweetheart," he said, "you shall never go; for that would be to give me my death-blow, and the most cruel death-blow of all. The first man that saw you would take you for his own; and, when I heard that, I should plunge my knife into my heart. No, I would not do that! I would run with all my might against a wall or a rock, and I would throw myself head first upon it, with such a plunge, that my eyes should spring out, and I would brain myself. I would rather by a hundred times die such a death, than know that you belonged to any other man!"

"Aucassin," replied Nicolette, "I do not believe that you love me as much as you say; but I am quite sure that I love you more than you love me."

"Never!" replied Aucassin. "Oh, my darling sweetheart! you cannot love me more than I love you. No woman can love man as man loves woman; for woman's love is in her eye, it is in the tip of her toe, and the end of her finger: but man's love is in the bottom of his heart, and so firmly does it grow there, that it can never be uprooted."

So did Aucassin and Nicolette talk together when the watchmen of the town came up by the next street, with their swords hidden under their cloaks.

Now, the Count Garin had bidden these people kill Nicolette if they could take her; and just as they were coming up where they would see her, and run to seize her, the lookout on the tower saw them.

"What a pity," cried he, "to kill so pretty a girl as this! It would be a mercy to warn her before these wretches see her. For, as soon as they kill her, my boy Aucassin will die; and that would be a pity, *certes!*"

[*Now they sing it.*]
Now, I tell you that this lookout
    Was as courteous as brave,
And so this song the man began,
    Poor Nicolette to save,—
"Oh, my pretty girl!" said he,
"Whose heart can beat so true and free,
Whose eyes are bright, whose form is light,
And whose face is so sweet to see,
    I know you're watching there
    For your lover underground;
    He weeps for you in his despair,
    Bolted, barred, and bound.
    Now, maiden, list to me:
    Of the night-watch beware,
    For they are passing by,
    A hidden sword on every thigh;
    Hide yourself as they pass by;
    Maiden, beware."

[*Now they speak it, and talk it, and tell it.*]

"Ah!" replied Nicolette to the lookout, "may God grant eternal repose to the souls of your father and of your mother for this kindly warning you have given to me! I will take care of the rascals, whoever they may be; and in this the good God will help me."

So saying, she wrapped herself in her mantle as closely as she could, and hid herself silently in the shadow of the pillar. So she waited till the watchmen had passed by; and, when she thought them far enough gone, she took leave of Aucassin, and went her way.

So she came to the castle walls. Now these were broken in many of the joints; and the active girl was able to let herself down, with the help of her hands, as a little four-footed kid would have done. But, when she was half-way down, she looked into the ditch, and she was frightened to see how sheer and steep it was.

"Oh, my dear Maker God!" she whispered, "if I let myself fall, I shall break my neck; if I stay where I am, they will seize me, and burn me: well, one death with another, I had rather run the risk of being killed than serve as a sight for all the people to-morrow."

So she made the sign of the cross, and let herself slide down the face of the wall to the very bottom of the ditch. Then she looked at her pretty feet and her pretty hands, which had never known what it was to be wounded before. They were all scratched and torn; and the blood flowed from them in a dozen places. But Nicolette felt no pain, because she was still so much afraid; for she had only succeeded in getting into the ditch, and now she must get out again.

The bold girl tried here, and she tried there; for she knew that it was a bad place to stay in; and at last she found one of the pointed stakes, which the defenders of the castle had thrown down on the besiegers when they were attacked. This she took, and with its aid she clambered up the reverse of the ditch, step after step. And soon she was at the top, though not without great pains.

The woods were two arbalist shots away from her,—woods which stretched thirty leagues this way, and thirty leagues that way, all haunted by wild beasts and venomous serpents. Poor Nicolette was frightened to death when she thought of them, because she did not want to be eaten alive; but still she pressed on, because she had no more wish to be burned alive.

      [Now they sing it.]
Nicolette, of lovely face,
  Clambered from the ditch so deep,
  And then began to wail and weep,
And to Jesus Christ to cry:—

   "Father, king of majesty,
     I do not know
     Where I shall go;
  For if, in flight, I should
  Lose me in the wood,
  The boars and lions grim
  Would tear me limb from limb;
But if men find me anywhere,
  And to the town I am returned,
They'll light a fire in the square,
And to the stake will tie me there,
  And my body will be burned.

"No, my God, no!
Hear me as I cry;
It shall not be so;
Better far that I
By the wolves be hunted down,
Than go captive to the town
So to die!

"I will not go."

[Now they tell it, and speak it, and talk it.]

Nicolette grieved, as you have heard, and then commended herself to God, and plunged into the woods, but did not dare go too far in, for fear of beasts and snakes.

She walked along for some time by the edge of the wood, frightened to death, starting at the slightest sound, and then going forward again with the utmost care. She walked this way and that, till she was so tired that she could walk no longer, and she lay down on a smooth bed of grass, and went to sleep; and there she slept till morning.

Early in the morning some shepherds passed by, on their way towards the town, as they were driving their sheep and herds to feed between the woods and the river. Now there was a fresh fountain near the place where Nicolette was lying; and it happened that the shepherds came to the fountain, and spread a cloak on the grass, and put their bread upon it, and sat down there for their simple breakfast.

While they were eating it, Nicolette was wakened by their talk, and by the song of the birds who were twittering in the branches.

She went to the shepherds, and spoke to the youngest of them, and said,—

"Pretty boy, may our Lady Mary take care of you!"

"May God bless you!" replied this young shepherd, whose speech came easier to him than the others.

"Pretty boy," said Nicolette, "do you know Aucassin, the son of Count Garin, of Beaucaire?"

"Oh, yes! we know him."

"As you would have God bless you, pretty boy, tell him that there is a strange wild beast in this wood; and that he ought to come out to hunt for her; and that, if he takes her, he would not give one of her limbs,—no, not for a hundred marks of gold, nor for five hundred marks, nor for all the gold that can be told."

As she said this, the shepherds were looking at Nicolette, and were wondering at her beauty.

"You speak false in saying this," said the shepherd, who had his tongue more at command than the others had; "for there is not in all this forest a single lion, or boar, or stag, or any other brute, so rare, that one of his limbs should be worth more than two deniers, or three at most. And you talk of such sums of money, that no one will believe a word you say. You are a fairy, and no human creature. We do not want your company; and so go your way."

"Ah, pretty boy!" said Nicolette again, "do what I bid you in the name of God; for the creature of which I speak to you has such power, that she can cure Aucassin of this trouble in which he is now. I have five sous in my purse, take them, and say to him, that, for three days, he must come to hunt for this creature in this forest; that, if he do not find her in three days at most, he will never be cured from his pain."

"By my faith!" said the young shepherd, "we will take your money. If Aucassin passes this way, we will tell him what you say; but we will not go to find him."

"God bless you!" said Nicolette. And so she bade the shepherds good-by courteously.

[Now they sing it.]

Nicolette, of lovely face,
  Bade the shepherd boys good-day,
And through the forest took her way,
  Till she came to a crossing-place,
Where seven roads met in the wood;
There, all alone, she thought it good
  Her lover's love to try.

She gathers store of *fleurs-de-lis*
    And thyme and brake,
    And many leaves,
    Her hut to make;
    And from all these she weaves
The prettiest hut your eyes did ever see.

  And then, by every saint above,
  The pretty builder swore,
    That, if her darling dear
    Should never enter here,
  She would not be his darling more,
    Nor should he be her love.

[Now they speak it, and talk it, and tell it.]

Nicolette having thus made her little hut, and thatched it thickly on the inside and on the outside with fresh leaves and fragrant flowers, hid herself under a bush to see what Aucassin would do.

Now the rumor ran through all the country that Nicolette was lost. Some said that she had escaped, and others said that the Count Garin had killed her.

If everybody else had been sure of this, Aucassin would not have been. But of this he gave no sign. And his father, well pleased to be rid of Nicolette, ordered that he should be released from prison, and bade all the knights and damsels of the country give *fêtes* for him, which might distract him.

The day when Nicolette disappeared, when the court of the count was crowded with knights and ladies, Aucassin was leaning against a pillar, all dejected, and out of his senses with sorrow, and only thinking of her he loved.

A knight who saw how melancholy he was came to him and said,—

"Aucassin, I have been sick of the same disease as you, so that I know how to give you good advice, if you will only hear me."

"Thank you, sir!" said Aucassin; "for indeed I am greatly in need of good advice and cure."

Then the knight said, "Mount your horse, and go into the woods yonder. The sight of the plains, the sweet odor of the plants, and the songs of the little birds will all comfort you, believe me."

"Thank you, indeed, sir!" said Aucassin. "I will gladly do so."

So he went out from the hall at once, and went down the steps, hurried to the stable, and put saddle and bridle on one of his horses, which was waiting there. He put his foot in the stirrup, sprang upon the noble beast, and rode out from the castle walls. Once outside, he remembered the advice which the knight had given to him, and went straight to the woods. Here he soon met the shepherds seated on the grass around the spring, eating their bread with great joy; for it was now noon.

[*Now they sing it.*]

All the shepherd-boys had met,
Esmeret and Martinet,
Johannot and Fruclinet,
Aubuget and Robecon.
By the spring they sat; and one
With the sweetest voice began,
"God bless Master Aucassin,
And the girl so fair and bright,
With teeth so white, and eyes so gray,
Who to us this blessed day
The money brought,
With which we bought
Cakes to eat, and pipes to play,
Flutes and horns and whittles good,
And heavy mauls to cleave the wood.
May God cure him!

    May God cure her!
      This is what I say."

[Now they tell it, and say it, and talk it.]

When Aucassin heard the shepherds singing this, he thought in a moment that his sweetheart Nicolette, his well-beloved, had passed that way. To make sure of this, he hastened to them.

"God bless you, my fine boys!" he cried.

"God care for you!" replied he whose speech came easiest to him.

"My good boys," said Aucassin, "sing me the song again which you were singing just now."

"No, my fine lord, we will not sing it again; and cursed be he who shall sing it to you!"

"My fine fellows, do you not know me?"

"We know you very well, sir: we know that you are Aucassin, our young gentleman. But we are not your men; we are the count's men."

"I beg you to do what I ask you."

"Why should I sing for you, if I do not choose to sing? It is very true that the Count of Garin is the richest man in all this country; but if he found one of my oxen or cows or sheep, in his grazing-lands or in his grain, he would make their eyes fly out. Why should I sing for you, then, if I choose to hold my tongue?"

"May God bless you, my boys!" said Aucassin again. "See, here are ten sols which I have found in my pocket. Take them, and sing to me again the song I heard you sing just now."

"Sir," said the shepherd, "I will take your money; but I will not sing to you, because I have sworn that I will not. I will do what I can; and I will tell it to you, if you please."

"*Pardieu!*" cried Aucassin, "I had rather hear your story than hear nothing."

"Sir," said the shepherd again, "we were sitting here by the spring, just as we are now. It was between the first hour and the third hour. We were eating our bread here, when there came up a girl who was the most beautiful creature in the world, so that we thought she was a fairy; for the whole wood was lighted up by her.

"She gave us so much of her money that we promised her that, if you passed by here, we would tell you that you must go and hunt in the forest; and that there was such a creature, that, if you caught her, you would not sell one of her joints,—no, not for five hundred marks of silver,—and also that you would be cured of your disease. She also said that, if you did not catch this creature before three days had passed, you would never see her. Go to the hunt, then, if you please, or do not go to the hunt, if you do not please: as to that, I have nothing to do. I have told my message."

"You have said quite enough, my boys," replied Aucassin. "God grant that I may meet her!"

[*Now they sing it.*]
Aucassin most gladly heard
Every sweet and loving word
Of his darling of the charming face:
   In his heart they pierced him so,
     That he left the shepherds good,
     And plunged into the deepest wood,
Where'er his horse might choose to go.

   "O Nicolette, my sweet!"
He sighed as sadly as before,
   "It is you I hope to meet:
I do not hunt nor deer or boar.
   In this forest black
   It is you I track,
That I this blessed day
   Your pretty smile may greet,
May see your pretty eyes of gray;
   See you, my darling sweet!
For oh! the Almighty I implore
That I may see your face once more,
   My dear!"

[*Now they tell it, and speak it, and talk it.*]

Aucassin wandered here and there in the forest, just as his horse might carry him. Do not think that the brambles and briers spared him. I can tell you that they tore his clothes so that he had hardly a rag left upon him. And the blood ran down his arms, his sides, and his legs, in thirty or forty different places; so that you might have tracked him in the wood by the red drops which he left on the grass wherever he went. But Aucassin was all the time thinking of his darling sweetheart Nicolette, so that he did not once feel any pain.

So he travelled through the forest all day long, without gaining any news of his beautiful sweetheart; and, when he saw the night coming on, he began to weep bitterly.

As he was riding along through an old path, where the bushes had grown up thick and high, he saw before him, right in the middle of the road, a man whom I will describe to you.

He was large, and marvellously ugly. His face was blacker than broiled meat, and it was so large that there was a palm-breadth between his two eyes. His cheeks were enormous; and so were his nostrils and his nose, which was flat; his lips were big, and redder than coals; and he had frightful great yellow teeth. He had on sandals of leather, and greaves of leather, which were tied with thongs up to his knees. He was covered with a great double cloak, and was resting on a heavy club.

Aucassin was frightened, and said to him, "Good brother, may God help you!"

"God bless you!" replied the other.

"What are you doing there?" said Aucassin.

"What affair is that of yours?"

"I only ask with good will."

"Well, why are you mourning and weeping so? If I were as rich a man as you are, I am sure nothing in the world would make me weep."

"How do you know me, then?"

"I know that you are Aucassin, the son of the count; and, if you will tell me why you weep, I will tell you why I am here."

"I am very glad to tell you. I came out to hunt this morning. I had a white harrier, the prettiest dog in the whole world; and I have lost him. That is the reason why I am weeping."

"What! For a miserable dog will you use the tears in your eyes or the heart in your breast? You are a poor creature to be weeping so—and you the richest man in the country! If your father wanted fifteen or twenty white harriers, he could have them in a minute. Now I am in sorrow for something real."

"What is that?"

"I am going to tell you, sir. I was hired by a rich farmer here to drive his cart, which was drawn by four oxen. It is three days since I lost the red ox, who was the finest of the four. I went here, and I went there; I left my wagon, and sought everywhere for the beast, but I could not find him. It is three days since I ate anything or drank anything; and here I stray about, for I do not dare go into the town. They would put me in prison; for I have nothing to pay with. All my wealth is what you see upon my body. I have a mother. She, poor woman, was not richer than I. All she had was an old petticoat to cover her poor old body; and they pulled that off her back, and now she is lying in the straw. That troubles me more than my condition. For money comes and goes. If I lose to-day, I will gain to-morrow; and, when I can pay for the ox, I will. I will never shed a tear for such a trifle as that. And here are you crying for a lost dog! You are a poor creature!"

"*Certes*, my good fellow, you are a good comforter," said Aucassin. "May God bless you! Tell me, how much was the red ox worth?"

"They charge me twenty sols for him, sir; nor can I beat them down a doit."

"Here are twenty sols which I have in my purse; take them, and pay for your ox."

"Thank you, indeed, sir!" said the man, "and may God send you that you are looking for!" So saying, he took leave; and Aucassin went on upon his way.

The night was fine and clear. Aucassin rode and rode for a long time; and after he had passed from one road to another, and from one path to another, he came at last to Nicolette's little lodge.

Inside and outside, before and behind, it had flowers marvellous sweet and lovely to the eye. A ray of moonlight lighted it up, so that Aucassin saw the pretty lodge, and stopped in a minute.

"Ah!" said he, "nobody but my darling Nicolette made this bower; and she has made it with her own pretty hands. For her sake and in memory of her I will dismount now; and I will spend the night here."

So saying, he took his foot from the stirrup, that he might dismount. But alas! he was thinking of nothing but Nicolette, and was taking no care of himself. Besides, his horse was large and was high; and so it happened that he fell upon a stone, and fell so hard that he put his shoulder out of joint.

All wounded as he was, still he was able to fasten the horse to a tree with his other arm. Then he went back to the lodge, and entered it, and lay upon his back, and looked up at the blue sky and the golden stars through a hole in the roof of his fragrant retreat. As he lay and looked, he saw one star brighter than all the others. Then, with a sigh, he began to sing.

[*Now they sing it.*]
Star of light, which I behold
  With the Queen of Light,
Nicolette of locks of gold
  Is with thee to-night.
      Oh! if I were there in bliss
       In thy still home above,
      How gladly would I pet and kiss
       My sweetest love!

[*Now they tell it, and speak it, and talk it.*]

When Nicolette heard Aucassin, she ran to him; for she was not far off. She entered the lodge, and threw her beautiful arms around his neck, kissed him, and embraced him most tenderly.

"Well found, dear sweet friend!" said she.

"And you, my darling, you are well found!" and so they kissed again and again with infinite joy.

"O my darling," said Aucassin, "my shoulder is sadly wounded. But, now I am with you, I know no pain nor grief."

Nicolette, when she heard this, felt of the place, and found, indeed, that the shoulder was out of joint. Then she tore a piece of linen, and placed in it a tuft of flowers and fresh herbs, and placed it on the sick place; and so she tended it and bandaged it with her white hands, that, with the aid of God, who cares for lovers, she cured him.

"Aucassin, my darling," said she, "what will you do now? If your father searches this wood to-morrow, he will find us. I do not know what will happen to you; but for me, I know I shall be killed."

"That is true, my darling," said Aucassin; "and that would be great grief to me: but, as long as I can, I will defend you and save you."

So saying, he mounted his horse, took his sweetheart before him, kissing her and embracing her; and so they rode across the country.

> [*Now they sing it.*]
> Aucassin, the handsome boy,
> Glad with love and quick with joy,
> Leaves this bower of their rest;
> Nicolette he fondly prest
>   In his arms upon his breast;
>   He folded fast his pretty prize,
>   Kissed her lips, and kissed her eyes,
>   Kissed her lovely face all over,—
>   Laughing boy and happy lover.

> But all this must not last.
>   "Dear Aucassin,"
>   The girl began,
>   "To what country shall we go?"
>   "Dear child," said he, "how should I know?
>   Little, dearest, do I care,
>   How we go, or when, or where,—
>   In this wood, or far away,
>   If from you I do not stray."
> Then mountains high they passed,
>   Passed through many lands,
> Till to the sea they found their way,
>   And stood upon the sands
>   By the shore.

[Now they tell it, and speak it, and talk it.]

Aucassin and his darling then dismounted. He took his horse by the bridle, and her by the hand, and so they walked along the beach. By and by they saw some sailors, and made signals to them, and the men landed, and agreed to take them back with them to the ship.

As soon as they were at sea, a terrible storm arose, so wonderful that it hurled them along from one country to another, till they came to a harbor at the castle of Torelore.[2] They asked what country it was, and were told it was the country of the King of Torelore. Then Aucassin asked if he were at war; and they said he was, and that it was a very cruel war. Then he thanked the sailors, and took leave of them; mounted his horse, with Nicolette before him, and so rode towards the castle.

[2] Torelore, or Turelure, so called, it is said, from the singularities of the people. Now, *Turelure* is the refrain of an old French song, which means, "*always the same*," as; we might say, "So, so, so, so, so." The place is *Aigues Mortes*, known to tourists, but now five or six miles from the sea. Aigues Mortes was originally *Aquæ Mortuæ*, the name of a land-locked seaport.—E. E. H.

"Where is the king?" said he.

"He is in bed," they said.

"And where is his wife?" said Aucassin.

"She is in the army, where she leads all the people of the country."

When Aucassin heard this, he was very much amazed. He went to the palace, dismounted with Nicolette, begged her to hold his horse, and, with his sword at his side, went to the king's chamber. There he pulled the clothes off the bed, and threw them into the middle of the room. Then he seized a stick, and beat the king so heartily that you would have thought he would kill him.

"Oh, oh, oh! my dear sir," cried the king. "What are you doing with me? Are you crazy, to beat a man so in his own house?"

"By the heart of God!" replied Aucassin, "I will kill you, misbegotten dog, if you do not swear that no man in this country shall ever lie in bed as you do."

The king took the oath; and Aucassin then said, "Now take me to the army, where your wife is."

"With pleasure," said the king.

Both went down to the court. The king mounted a horse, Aucassin mounted his own; Nicolette took refuge in the queen's chamber; and both the men went to the army. When they arrived, the battle was in all its fury. The battle was fought with wild apples, eggs, and green cheeses.

Aucassin, of noble blood,
By the battling armies stood,
   And wondered at the sight;
For men-at-arms were seen
   Keeping up the fight:
With eggs they threw, with all their might,
Apples raw and cheeses green!
   And the soldier who with these
   Most disturbed the fountain bright,
   He was deemed the bravest knight.
Aucassin, of noble blood,
Watched this battle where he stood,
   And laughed outright.

[*Now they tell it, and speak it, and talk it.*]

Aucassin went to the king, and said to him, "Are these your enemies, sir?"

"Yes," replied the king.

"Do you wish to have me avenge you?"

"Indeed I do!"

Then Aucassin drew his sword, plunged into the thick of the fight, and cut and thrust from right to left; so that in almost no time he had killed a great number.

"My dear sir," cried the king, seizing Aucassin's horse by the bridle, "do not kill them in this way!"

"How else can I avenge you?" said Aucassin.

"Sir, you do too much. It is not our custom to kill each other in this fashion: all that we do is to put the enemy to flight."

Then they returned to the Castle of Torelore, where the people of the country advised the king to drive Aucassin out of his land, and to keep this pretty girl Nicolette for his wife; for she seemed to them a lady of high degree.

When Nicolette heard this, she was sorely grieved, and said,—

[*Now they sing it.*]

"Sire, king of Torelore,
Puissant prince and lord of glory,"
   Said the pretty Nicolette,
"You think me like a fool in story:
I am not one yet.
   Aucassin shall I forget,
   Who loves me as his own?
Not all your shows and dances proud,
Not all your harps and viols loud,
   Are worth my dear alone."

Aucassin and his darling Nicolette took great delight and ease in the Castle of Torelore.

While they were there, some Saracens came up by sea, who assaulted the castle, and took it by storm. As soon as they had taken it, they carried off the people prisoners. They put Nicolette into one ship, and Aucassin into another, tied hand and foot. Then they set sail again.

As they sailed, a violent storm arose; and the ships were separated from each other. The ship in which Aucassin was was thrown so far at the mercy of the waves that at last she came to the Castle of Beaucaire.

The people of that country ran to the harbor; and when they recognized Aucassin, they were very happy, for he had been away for three years, and his father and mother were dead. They took him in triumph to the Castle of Beaucaire, and acknowledged him as their lord and master in place of the Count Garin. He took possession of his lands in peace.

[Now they sing it.]

Aucassin did repair
To his town of Beaucaire,
   And well governed kingdom and city.
How glad would he be,
If he only could see
   His own Nicolette so pretty!

   "Dear child of sweet face,
     How I wish that I knew
   To what sort of place
     I must go to find you!
There is no land or sea
     God has made here below,
Where to look after thee
     I would not gladly go."

[Now they tell it, they speak it, and talk it.]

We will leave Aucassin there, that we may tell about Nicolette.

The ship on which she had been taken away was that of the King of Carthage and his twelve brothers, who were princes and kings like himself. When they saw how beautiful Nicolette was, they did her great honor, and asked who she was; for she seemed to them a noble lady of high degree. But she could give them no account of herself, having been carried from home when she was a very little girl.

Soon they came to Carthage. As soon as they saw the walls of the castle, and all the country round about, Nicolette recollected that it was here that she had been nursed, and had grown up, and that it was here where she had been taken as a slave; for she had not been so young but she remembered perfectly well that she had been daughter of the King of Carthage.

[*Now they sing it.*]

The wise Nicolette
  Walks up on the shores,
And she does not forget
  The castles and towers.
    At first, the grand sight
    Filled the child with delight,
    Then she sighed, "Well-a-day!
    What would Aucassin say,
    My own darling knight,
If he knew that the pirates, that terrible day,
The Princess of Carthage had carried away?

  "Dear boy, thy heart's love
  Brings me sorrow and pain;
May the good God above
  Let me see thee again!
    Come, fold me in thine own embrace,
    Kiss my lips, and kiss my eyes,
    Kiss again your sweetheart's face!"
      So his princess sadly cries
    To her lord and lover.

When Nicolette sang this, the King of Carthage heard her.

"My dear child," he cried, throwing his arms around her neck, "tell me who you are, I beg you! Do not be afraid of me."

"Sir," replied Nicolette, "I am the daughter of the King of Carthage, from whom I was stolen fifteen years ago."

It was easy for the king and his brothers to see that what Nicolette said was true. So they took her to the palace, and made a great *fête* for her, as was fitting for the daughter of a king. They wished to give her for a wife to a king of the pagans; but she refused. She said she did not yet wish to marry.

After three or four days, she thought of the way by which she could gain some news of Aucassin. The only way she could think of was to learn to play the violin; and one day, when they wanted to marry her to a rich pagan prince, she ran away, and came to the harbor, where she lodged with a poor old woman who lived there. Then she took a certain herb, and squeezed the juice out of it; and with this juice she stained her pretty face from top to bottom, so that all of a sudden it became quite black. Then she made herself a tunic, a mantle, shirt, and breeches, and so disguised herself as a minstrel; took her violin, and went to a sailor, who, with some hesitation, agreed to take her into his ship.

The sails were already set; and so swiftly did the ship sail here and there through the high sea, that she arrived at the country of Provence; and there Nicolette landed with her violin. Once on land, the gentle girl began wandering through the country, playing her violin as she went from this place to that, until she came to the Castle of Beaucaire, where was Aucassin.

[Now they sing it.]

Aucassin is sitting there
At his castle at Beaucaire;
All his barons brave surround him,
Sweet the flowers and birds around him:
But he is in despair.
    For Aucassin cannot forget
    His charming Nicolette,
    His darling fair.
While he sighs, the girl has found him;
For she stands upon the stair,
Deftly tunes her viol-strings,
And to the prince and barons sings:—

"Wise and loyal knights,
Hear my little lay:
How Nicolette and Aucassin were kept so far apart,
While he loved her, as she loved him, with all his heart,
As you do not love every day.

"One day the pagans made her slave
In the tower of Torelore.
Where was Aucassin the brave?
I do not know his story.
But Nicolette, of whom I sing,
Where she has her father found,
And where he reigns as king.
He would give the maiden over
To wed in pomp a pagan lover.
    But Nicolette says, No!
    She loves a damoiseau,
    Named Aucassin, and so
    She will wed no pagan hound,
    She waits alone till she has found
        Him whom she loves."

[Now they tell it, and speak it, and talk it.]

When Aucassin heard Nicolette sing this, he was full of joy. He led her on one side, and said,—

"My good fellow, do you know anything more of this Nicolette, whose story you have been singing to us?"

"Yes, sir: I know that she is the most constant, and the wisest creature that ever was born, as well as the most beautiful. She is the daughter of the King of Carthage, from whom she was stolen in her childhood; and he, in turn, took her and Aucassin from the Castle of Torelore. Glad was he, indeed, to find her; and now he wants to marry her to one of the mightiest kings of Spain. But Nicolette would rather be hanged and burned than consent to be the wife of any but Aucassin, though she were asked to wed the most powerful and the richest prince in the earth."

"My good fellow," cried Aucassin, "if you could only return to the country where Nicolette now is, and tell her that I beg her to come here to speak to me, I would gladly give you all you could ask, or all you could take of what I have. For love of her, I shall take no other wife, of however high degree; for I shall never have any except her, whom here I wait for, and whom I should have gone to seek, had I only known where to find her."

"Sir, if you have thus determined, I will go and seek Nicolette, for your sake and for her sake, for I love her truly."

Then Aucassin swore that this was his dearest thought and wish; and he gave to the minstrel twenty livres.

As the minstrel turned away, she saw that he was weeping, so strong was his passion.

So she turned on her steps, and said, "Do not be distressed, sir. I promise you I will bring her before long."

Aucassin thanked her; and Nicolette at once withdrew, and went to the house of the viscountess, the wife of the viscount, her godfather. He was dead. At this house Nicolette lodged: she made a confidante of his widow, and told her the whole story.

Her mistress recognized her readily as being the Nicolette whom she had educated. She bade her wash herself and bathe, and rest for a week. Then she anointed her face with the juice of a certain herb she knew; and she did this so often and so well that Nicolette again became as beautiful as ever.

When all this was done, Nicolette dressed herself in rich robes of silk, of which the lady had ample provision. Then she seated herself upon a sofa of the same stuff, and sent her hostess to seek her friend.

The viscountess came to the palace, where she found Aucassin, who was weeping and wailing for his darling Nicolette, who was too long in coming, as he said.

"Aucassin," said the lady to him, "do not lament any longer, but come with me. I will show you the thing which you love best in all the world; that is Nicolette, your sweetheart dear, who has come from distant lands to join you again."

Aucassin was very happy.

[*Now they sing it.*]

When Aucassin has heard
This lady's welcome word,
   That the girl of lovely face,
   His sweetheart dear, had come
       To that place,
   He comes as quick as wind
   With this lady who could find
    Her in her home.

   He comes into the room
   Where his darling has her seat.
   When she sees the boy appear,
   Quickly to his arms she flies
   To kiss his lips, and kiss his eyes,
   Her only love, her only dear,
   And give him welcome sweet.

   So the evening sped away;
   And on the morning of another day
   She was espoused to him there,
   And so became the Lady of Beaucaire.
   To both long days of pleasure came,—
   Pleasure that was aye the same;
   Nicolette, the happy she,
   And Aucassin, the happy he.

   And here will end my little lay,
   Because I've nothing more to say.

THE LOST PALACE.

"Passengers for Philadelphia and New York will change cars."

This annoying and astonishing cry was loudly made in the palace-car "City of Thebes," at Pittsburg, just as the babies were well asleep, and all the passengers adapting themselves to a quiet evening.

"Impossible!" said I mildly to the "gentlemanly conductor," who beamed before me in the majesty of gilt lace on his cap, and the embroidered letters P. P. C. These letters do not mean, as in French, "to take leave," for the peculiarity of this man is, that he does not leave you till your journey's end: they mean, in American, "Pullman's Palace Car." "Impossible!" said I; "I bought my ticket at Chicago through to Philadelphia, with the assurance that the palace-car would go through. This lady has done the same for herself and her children. Nay, if you remember, you told me yourself that the 'City of Thebes' was built for the Philadelphia service, and that I need not move my hat, unless I wished, till we were there."

The man did not blush, but answered, in the well-mannered tone of a subordinate used to obey, "Here are my orders, sir; telegram just received here from head-quarters: '"City of Thebes" is to go to Baltimore.' Another palace here, sir, waiting for you." And so we were trans-shipped into such chairs and berths as might have been left in this other palace, as not wanted by anybody in the great law of natural selection; and the "City of Thebes" went to Baltimore, I suppose. The promises which had been made to us when we bought our tickets went to their place, and the people who made them went to theirs.

Except for this little incident, of which all my readers have probably experienced the like in these days of travel, the story I am now to tell would have seemed to me essentially improbable. But so soon as I reflected, that, in truth, these palaces go hither, go thither, controlled or not, as it may be, by some distant bureau, the story recurred to me as having elements of *vraisemblance* which I had not noticed before. Having occasion, nearly at the same time, to inquire at the Metropolitan station in Boston for a lost shawl which had been left in a certain Brookline car, the gentlemanly official told me that he did not know where that car was; he had not heard of it for several days. This again reminded me of "The Lost Palace." Why should not one palace, more or less, go astray, when there are thousands to care for? Indeed, had not Mr. Firth told me, at the Albany, that the worst difficulty in the administration of a strong railway is, that they cannot call their freight-cars home? They go astray on the line of some weaker sister, which finds it convenient to use them till they begin to show a need for paint or repairs. If freight-cars disappear, why not palaces? So the story seems to me of more worth, and I put it upon paper.

It was on my second visit to Melbourne that I heard it. It was late at night, in the coffee-room of the Auckland Arms, rather an indifferent third-class house, in a by-street in that city, to which, in truth, I should not have gone had my finances been on a better scale than they were. I laid down at last an old New-York Herald, which the captain of the "Osprey" had given me that morning, and which, in the hope of home-news, I had read and read again to the last syllable of the "personals." I put down the paper as one always puts down an American paper in a foreign land, saying to myself, "Happy is that nation whose history is unwritten." At that moment Sir Roger Tichborne, who had been talking with an intelligent-looking American on the other side of the table, stretched his giant form, and said he believed he would play a game of billiards before he went to bed. He left us alone; and the American crossed the room, and addressed me.

"You are from Massachusetts, are you not?" said he. I said I had lived in that State.

"Good State to come from," said he. "I was there myself for three or four months,—four months and ten days precisely. Did not like it very well; did not like it. At least, I liked it well enough: my wife did not like it; she could not get acquainted."

"Does she get acquainted here?" said I, acting on a principle which I learned from Scipio Africanus at the Latin School, and so carrying the war into the enemy's regions promptly. That is to say, I saw I must talk with this man, and I preferred to have him talk of his own concerns than of mine.

"O sir, I lost her,—I lost her ten years ago! Lived in New Altoona then. I married this woman the next autumn, in Vandalia. Yes, Mrs. Joslyn is very well satisfied here. She sees a good deal of society, and enjoys very good health."

I said that most people did who were fortunate enough to have it to enjoy. But Mr. Joslyn did not understand this bitter sarcasm, far less resent it. He went on, with sufficient volubility, to give to me his impressions of the colony,—of the advantages it would derive from declaring its independence, and then from annexing itself to the United States. At the end of one of his periods, goaded again to say something, I asked why he left his own country for a "colony," if he so greatly preferred the independent order of government.

Mr. Joslyn looked round somewhat carefully, shut the door of the room in which we were now alone,—and were likely, at that hour of the night, to be alone,—and answered my question at length, as the reader will see.

"Did you ever hear of the lost palace?" said he a little anxiously.

I said, no; that, with every year or two, I heard that Mr. Layard had found a palace at Nineveh, but that I had never heard of one's being lost.

"They don't tell of it, sir. Sometimes I think they do not know themselves. Does not that seem possible?" And the poor man repeated this question with such eagerness, that, in spite of my anger at being bored by him, my heart really warmed toward him. "I really think they do not know. I have never seen one word in the papers about it. Now, they would have put something in the papers,—do you not think they would? If they knew it themselves, they would."

"Knew what?" said I, really startled out of my determination to snub him.

"Knew where the palace is,—knew how it was lost."

By this time, of course, I supposed he was crazy. But a minute more dispelled that notion; and I beg the reader to relieve his mind from it. This man knew perfectly well what he was talking about, and never, in the whole narration, showed any symptom of mania,—a matter on which I affect to speak with the intelligence of the "experts" indeed.

After a little of this fencing with each other, in which he satisfied himself that my ignorance was not affected, he took a sudden resolution, as if it were a relief to him to tell me the whole story.

"It was years on years ago," said he. "It was when they first had palaces."

Still thinking of Nimrod's palace and Priam's, I said that must have been a great while ago.

"Yes, indeed," said he. "You would not call them palaces now, since you have seen Pullman's and Wagner's. But we called them palaces then. So many looking-glasses, you know, and tapestry carpets and gold spit-boxes. Ours was the first line that run palaces."

I asked myself, mentally, of what metal were the spit-boxes in Semiramis' palace; but I said nothing.

"Our line was the first line that had them. We were running our lightning express on the 'Great Alleghanian.' We were in opposition to everybody, made close connections, served supper on board, and our passengers only were sure of the night-boat at St. Louis. Those were the days of river-boats, you know. We introduced the palace feature on the railroad; and very successful it was. I was an engineer. I had a first-rate character, and the best wages of any man on the line. Never put me on a dirt-dragger or a lazy freight loafer, I tell you. No, sir! I ran the expresses, and nothing else, and lay off two days in the week, besides. I don't think I should have thought of it but for Todhunter, who was my palace conductor."

Again this IT, which had appeared so mysteriously in what the man said before. I asked no question, but listened, really interested now, in the hope I should find out what IT was; and this the reader will learn. He went on, in a hurried way:—

"Todhunter was my palace conductor. One night he was full, and his palace was hot, and smelled bad of whale-oil. We did not burn petroleum then. Well, it was a splendid full moon in August; and we were coming down grade, making the time we had lost at the Brentford Junction. Seventy miles an hour she ran if she ran one. Todhunter had brought his cigar out on the tender, and was sitting by me. Good Lord! it seems like last week.

"Todhunter says to me, 'Joslyn,' says he, 'what's the use of crooking all round these valleys, when it would be so easy to go across?'

"You see, we were just beginning to crook round, so as to make that long bend there is at Chamoguin; but right across the valley we could see the stern lights of Fisher's train: it was not more than half a mile away, but we should run eleven miles before we came there."

I knew what Mr. Joslyn meant. To cross the mountain ranges by rail, the engineers are obliged to wind up one side of a valley, and then, boldly crossing the head of the ravine on a high arch, to wind up the other side still, so that perhaps half an hour's journey is consumed, while not a mile of real distance is made. Joslyn took out his pencil, and on the back of an envelope drew a little sketch of the country; which, as it happened, I still preserve, and which, with his comments, explains his whole story completely. "Here we are," said he. "This black line is the Great Alleghanian,—double track, seventy pounds to the yard; no figuring off there, I tell you. This was a good straight run, down grade a hundred and seventy-two feet on the mile. There, where I make this X, we came on the Chamoguin Valley, and turned short, nearly north. So we ran wriggling about till Drums here, where we stopped if they showed lanterns,—what we call a flag-station. But there we got across the valley, and worked south again to this other X, which was, as I say, not five eighths of a mile from this X above, though it had taken us eleven miles to get there."

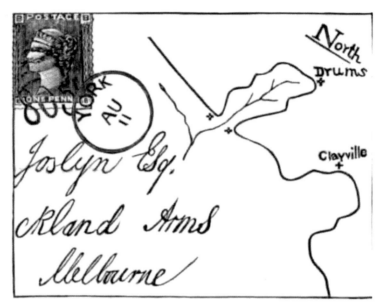

He had said it was not more than half a mile; but this half-mile grew to five eighths as he became more accurate and serious.

"Well," said he, now resuming the thread of his story, "it was Todhunter put it into my head. He owns he did. Todhunter says, says he, 'Joslyn, what's the use of crooking round all these valleys, when it would be so easy to go across?'

"Well, sir, I saw it then, as clear as I see it now. When that trip was done, I had two days to myself,—one was Sunday,—and Todhunter had the same; and he came round to my house. His wife knew mine, and we liked them. Well, we fell talking about it; and I got down the Cyclopædia, and we found out there about the speed of cannon-balls, and the direction they had to give them. You know this was only talk then; we never thought what would come of it; but very curious it all was."

And here Mr. Joslyn went into a long mathematical talk, with which I will not harass the reader, perfectly sure, from other experiments which I have tried with other readers, that this reader would skip it all if it were written down. Stated very briefly, it amounted to this: In the old-fashioned experiments of those days, a cannon-ball travelled four thousand and one hundred feet in nine seconds. Now, Joslyn was convinced, like every other engineman I ever talked to, that on a steep down-grade he could drive a train at the rate of a hundred miles an hour. This is thirteen hundred and fourteen feet in nine seconds,—almost exactly one third of the cannon-ball's velocity. At those

94

rates, if the valley at Chamoguin were really but five eighths of a mile wide, the cannon-ball would cross it in seven or eight seconds, and the train in about twenty-three seconds. Both Todhunter and Joslyn were good enough mechanics and machinists to know that the rate for thirty-three hundred feet, the width of the valley, was not quite the same as that for four thousand feet; for which, in their book, they had the calculations and formulas; but they also knew that the difference was to their advantage, or the advantage of the bold experiment which had occurred to both of them when Todhunter had made on the tender his very critical suggestion.

The reader has already conceived the idea of this experiment. These rash men were wondering already whether it were not possible to leap an engine flying over the Chamoguin ravine, as Eclipse or Flying Childers might have leaped the brook at the bottom of it. Joslyn believed implicitly, as I found in talk with him, the received statement of conversation, that Eclipse, at a single bound, sprang forty feet. "If Eclipse, who weighed perhaps one thousand two hundred, would spring forty feet, could not my train, weighing two hundred tons, spring a hundred times as far?" asked he triumphantly. At least, he said that he said this to Todhunter. They went into more careful studies of projectiles, to see if it could or could not.

The article on "Gunnery" gave them just one of those convenient tables which are the blessing of wise men and learned men, and which lead half-trained men to their ruin. They found that for their "range," which was, as they supposed, eleven hundred yards, the elevation of a forty-two pounder was one degree and a third; of a nine-pounder, three degrees. The elevation for a railway train, alas! no man had calculated. But this had occurred to both of them from the beginning. In descending the grade, at the spot where, on his little map, Joslyn made the more westerly X, they were more than eleven hundred feet above the spot where he had made his second, or easterly X. All this descent was to the advantage of the experiment. A gunner would have said that the first X "commanded" the second X, and that a battery there would inevitably silence a battery at the point below.

"We need not figure on it," said Todhunter, as Mrs. Joslyn called them in to supper. "If we did, we should make a mistake. Give me your papers. When I go up, Monday night, I'll give them to my brother Bill. I shall pass him at Faber's Mills. He has studied all these things, of course; and he will like the fun of making it out for us." So they sat down to Mrs. Joslyn's waffles; and, but for Bill Todhunter, this story would never have been told to me, nor would John Joslyn and "this woman" ever have gone to Australia.

But Bill Todhunter was one of those acute men of whom the new civilization of this country is raising thousands with every year; who, in the midst of hard hand-work, and a daily duty which to collegians, and to the ignorant men among their professors, seems repulsive, carry on careful scientific study, read the best results of the latest inquiry, manage to bring together a first-rate library of reference, never spend a cent for liquor or tobacco, never waste an hour at a circus or a ball, but make their wives happy by sitting all the evening, "figuring," one side of the table, while the wife is hemming napkins on the other. All of a sudden, when such a man is wanted, he steps out, and bridges the Gulf of Bothnia; and people wonder, who forget that for two centuries and a half the foresighted men and women of this country have been building up, in the face of the Devil of Selfishness on the one hand, and of the Pope of Rome on the other, a system of popular education, improving every hour.

At this moment Bill Todhunter was foreman of Repair Section No. 11 on the "Great Alleghanian,"—a position which needed a man of first-rate promptness, of great resource, of good education in engineering. Such a man had the "Great Alleghanian" found in him, by good luck; and they had promoted him to their hardest-worked and best-paid section,—the section an which, as it happened, was this Chamoguin run, and the long bend which I have described, by which the road "headed" that stream.

The younger Todhunter did meet his brother at Faber's Mills, where the repair-train had hauled out of the way of the express, and where the express took wood. The brothers always looked for each other on such occasions; and Bill promised to examine the paper which Joslyn had carefully written out, and which his brother brought to him.

I have never repeated in detail the mass of calculations which Bill Todhunter made on the suggestion thus given to him. If I had, I would not repeat them here, for a reason which has been suggested already. He became fascinated with the problem presented to him. Stated in the language of the craft, it was this:—

"Given a moving body, with a velocity eight thousand eight hundred feet in a minute, what should be its elevation that it may fall eleven hundred feet in the transit of five eighths of a mile?" He had not only to work up the parabola, comparatively simple, but he had to allow for the resistance of the air, on the supposition of a calm, according to the really admirable formulas of Robins and Coulomb, which were the best he had access to. Joslyn brought me one day a letter from Bill Todhunter, which shows how carefully he went into this intricate inquiry.

Unfortunately for them all, it took possession of this spirited and accomplished young man. You see, he not only had the mathematical ability for the calculation of the fatal curve, but, as had been ordered without any effort of his, he was in precisely the situation of the whole world for trying in practice his own great experiment. At each of the two X X of Joslyn's map, the company had, as it happened, switches for repair-trains or wood-trains. Had it not, Bill Todhunter had ample power to make them.

For the "experiment," all that was necessary was, that under the pretext of re-adjusting these switches, he should lay out that at the upper X so that it should run, on the exact grade which he required, to the western edge of the ravine, in a line which should be the direct continuation of the long, straight run with which the little map begins.

An engine, then, running down that grade at the immense rapidity practicable there, would take the switch with its full speed, would fly the ravine at precisely the proper slopes, and, if the switch had been rightly aligned, would land on the similar switch at the lower X. It would come down exactly right on the track, as you sit precisely on a chair when you know exactly how high it is.

"If." And why should it not be rightly aligned, if Bill Todhunter himself aligned it? This he was well disposed to do. He also would align the lower switch, that at the lower X, that it might receive into its willing embrace the engine on its arrival.

When the bold engineer had conceived this plan, it was he who pushed the others on to it, not they who urged him. They were at work on their daily duty, sometimes did not meet each other for a day or two. Bill Todhunter did not see them more than once in a fortnight. But whenever they did meet, the thing seemed to be taken more and more for granted. At last Joslyn observed one day, as he ran down, that there was a large working-party at the switch above Drums, and he could see Bill Todhunter, in his broad sombrero, directing them all. Joslyn was not surprised, somehow, when he came to the lower switch, to find another working-party there. The next time they all three met, Bill Todhunter told them that all was ready if they were. He said that he had left a few birches to screen the line of the upper switch, for fear some nervous bungler, driving an engine down, might be frightened, and "blow" about the switch. But he said that any night when the others were ready to make the fly, he was; that there would be a full moon the next Wednesday, and, if there was no wind, he hoped they would do it then.

"You know," said poor Joslyn, describing it to me, "I should never have done it alone; August would never have done it alone; no, I do not think that Bill Todhunter himself would have done it alone. But our heads were full of it. We had thought of it and thought of it till we did not think of much else; and here was everything ready, and neither of us was afraid, and neither of us chose to have the others think he was afraid. I did say, what was the truth, that I had never meant to try it with a train. I had only thought that we should apply to the supe, and that he would get up a little excursion party of gentlemen,—editors, you know, and stockholders,—who would like to do it together, and that I should have the pleasure and honor of taking them over. But Todhunter poohed at that. He said all the calculations were made for the inertia of a full train, that that was what the switch was graded for, and that everything would have to be altered if any part of the plan were altered. Besides, he said the superintendent would never agree, that he would insist on consulting the board and the chief engineer, and that they would fiddle over it till Christmas.

"'No,' said Bill, 'next Wednesday, or never! If you will not do it then, I will put the tracks back again.' August Todhunter said nothing; but I knew he would do what we agreed to, and he did.

"So at last I said I would jump it on Wednesday night, if the night was fine. But I had just as lief own to you that I hoped it would not be fine. Todhunter —Bill Todhunter, I mean—was to leave the switch open after the freight had passed, and to drive up to the Widow Jones's Cross Road. There he would have a lantern, and I would stop and take him up. He had a right to stop us, as chief of repairs. Then we should have seven miles down-grade to get up our speed, and then—we should see!"

"Mr. Ingham, I might have spared myself the hoping for foul weather. It was the finest moonlight night that you ever knew in October. And if Bill Todhunter had weighed that train himself, he could not have been better pleased,—one baggage-car, one smoking-car, two regular first-class, and two palaces: she run just as steady as an old cow! We came to the Widow Jones's, square on time; and there was Bill's lantern waving. I slowed the train: he jumped on the tender without stopping it. I 'up brakes' again, and then I told Flanagan, my fireman, to go back to the baggage-car, and see if they would lend me some tobacco. You see, we wanted to talk, and we didn't want him to see. 'Mr. Todhunter and I will feed her till you come back,' says I to Flanagan. In a minute after he had gone, August Todhunter came forward on the engine; and, I tell you, she did fly!

"'Not too fast,' said Bill, 'not too fast: too fast is as bad as too slow.'

"'Never you fear me,' says I. 'I guess I know this road and this engine. Take out your watch, and time the mile-posts,' says I; and he timed them. 'Thirty-eight seconds,' says he; 'thirty-seven and a half, thirty-six, thirty-six, thirty-six,'—three times thirty-six, as we passed the posts, just as regular as an old clock! And then we came right on the mile-post you know at Old Flander's. 'Thirty-six,' says Bill again. And then she took the switch,—I can hear that switch-rod ring under us now, Mr. Ingham,—and then—we were clear!

"Was not it grand? The range was a little bit up, you see, at first; but it seemed as if we were flying just straight across. All the rattle of the rail stopped, you know, though the pistons worked just as true as ever; neither of us said one word, you know; and she just flew—well, as you see a hawk fly sometimes, when he pounces, you know, only she flew so straight and true! I think you may have dreamed of such things. I have; and now,—now I dream it very often. It was not half a minute, you know, but it seemed a good long time. I said nothing and they said nothing; only Bill just squeezed my hand. And just as I knew we must be half over,—for I could see by the star I was watching ahead that we were not going up, but were falling again,—do you think the rope by my side tightened quick, and the old bell on the engine gave one savage bang, turned right over as far as the catch would let it, and stuck where it turned! Just that one sound, everything else was still; and then she landed on the rails, perhaps seventy feet inside the ravine, took the rails as true and sweet as you ever saw a ship take the water, hardly touched them, you know, skimmed—well, as I have seen a swallow skim on the sea; the prettiest, well, the tenderest touch, Mr. Ingham, that ever I did see! And I could just hear the connecting rods tighten the least bit in the world behind me, and we went right on.

"We just looked at each other in the faces, and we could not speak; no, I do not believe we spoke for three quarters of a minute. Then August said, 'Was not that grand? Will they let us do it always, Bill?' But we could not talk then. Flanagan came back with the tobacco, and I had just the wit to ask him why he had been gone so long. Poor fellow! he was frightened enough when we pulled up at Clayville, and he thought it was Drums. Drums, you see, was way up the bend, a dozen miles above Clayville. Poor Flanagan thought we must have passed there while he was skylarking in the baggage-car, and that he had not minded it. We never stopped at Drums unless we had passengers, or they. It was what we call a flag-station. So I blew Flanagan up, and told him he was gone too long.

"Well, sir, at Clayville we did stop,—always stopped there for wood. August Todhunter, he was the palace conductor; he went back to look to his passengers. Bill stayed with me. But in a minute August came running back, and called me off the engine. He led me forward, where it was dark; but I could see, as we went, that something was to pay. The minute we were alone he says,—

"'John, we've lost the rear palace.'

"'Don't fool me, August,' says I.

"'No fooling, John,' says he. 'The shackle parted. The cord parted, and is flying loose behind now. If you want to see, come and count the cars. The "General Fremont" is here all right; but I tell you the "James Buchanan" is at the bottom of the Chamoguin Creek.'

"I walked back to the other end of the platform, as fast as I could go, and not be minded. Todhunter was there before me, tying up the loose end of the bell-cord. There was a bit of the broken end of the shackle twisted in with the bolt. I pulled the bolt, and threw the iron into the swamp, far as I could fling her. Then I nodded to Todhunter, and walked forward, just as that old goose at Clayville had got his trousers on, so he could come out, and ask me if we were not ahead of time. I tell you, sir, I did not stop to talk with him. I just rang 'All aboard!' and started her again; and this time I run slow enough to save the time before we came down to Steuben. We were on time, all right, there."

Here poor Joslyn stopped a while in his story; and I could see that he was so wrought up with excitement that I had better not interrupt, either with questions or with sympathy. He rallied in a minute or two, and said,—

"I thought—we all thought—that there would be a despatch somewhere waiting us. But no; all was as regular is the clock. One palace more or less,—what did they know, and what did they care? So daylight came. We could not say a word, you know, with Flanagan there; and he only stopped, you know, a minute or two every hour; and just then was when August Todhunter had to be with his passengers, you know. Was not I glad when we came into Pemaquid,—our road ran from Pemaquid across the mountains to Eden, you know,—when we came into Pemaquid, and nobody had asked any questions?

"I reported my time at the office of the master of trains, and I went home. I tell you, Mr. Ingham, I have never seen Pemaquid Station since thatday.

"I had done nothing wrong, of course. I had obeyed every order, and minded every signal. But still I knew public opinion might be against me when they heard of the loss of the palace. I did not feel very well about it, and I wrote a note to say I was not well enough to take my train the next night; and I and Mrs. Joslyn went to New York, and I went aboard a Collins steamer as fireman; and Mrs. Joslyn, she went as stewardess; and I wrote to Pemaquid, and gave up my place. It was a good place, too; but I gave it up, and I left America.

"Bill Todhunter, he resigned his place too, that same day, though that was a good place. He is in the Russian service now. He is running their line from Archangel to Astrachan; good pay, he says, but lonely. August would not stay in America after his brother left; and he is now captain's clerk on the Harkaway steamers between Bangkok and Cochbang; good place, he says, but hot. So we are all parted.

"And do you know, sir, never one of us ever heard of the lost palace!"

Sure enough, under that very curious system of responsibility, by which one corporation owns the carriages which another corporation uses, nobody in the world has to this moment ever missed "The Lost Palace." On each connecting line, everybody knew that "she" was not there; but no one knew or asked where she was. The descent into the rocky bottom of the Chamoguin, more than fifteen hundred feet below the line of flight, had of course been rapid,— slow at first, but in the end rapid. In the first second, the lost palace had fallen sixteen feet; in the second, sixty-four; in the third, one hundred and forty-four; in the fourth, two hundred and fifty-six; in the fifth, four hundred feet; so that it must have been near the end of the sixth second of its fall, that, with a velocity now of more than six hundred feet in a second, the falling palace, with its unconscious passengers, fell upon the rocks at the bottom of the Chamoguin ravine. In the dead of night, wholly without jar or parting, those passengers must have been sleeping soundly; and it is impossible, therefore, on any calculation of human probability, that any one of them can have been waked an instant before the complete destruction of the palace, by the sudden shock of its fall upon the bed of the stream. To them the accident, if it is fair to call it so, must have been wholly free from pain.

The tangles of that ravine, and the swamp below it, are such that I suppose that even the most adventurous huntsman never finds his way there. On the only occasion when I ever met Mr. Jules Verne, he expressed a desire to descend there from one of his balloons, to learn whether the inhabitants of "The Lost Palace" might not still survive, and be living in a happy republican colony there,—a place without railroads, without telegrams, without mails, and certainly without palaces. But at the moment when these sheets go to press, no account of such an adventure has appeared from his rapid pen.

THE WESTERN GINEVRA.

CHAPTER I.

BOUGHT.

As pretty a girl as there was in Ohio. And how much that says!

Brunette, or of that tendency, yet with blue eyes. And how much that says!

Tall and strong, not too plump, but still not scrawny, nor as a skeleton in clothing. I do not say that she could whip her weight in wild-cats; I do not know. Of that breed of animals few are left in Ohio, thanks to the prowess of the grandmothers of the present generation. But I do say that of the mother of the mother of Hester Bryan, of whom I write, this eulogy was simple truth. The *Puma concolor*, or native catamount of those regions, had yielded a hundred times before her prowess. And this I will add,—that Hester Bryan was just a bit taller and prettier than her mother, as she, in her day, was taller and prettier than hers. For there are worlds of life in which

> "Nature gives us more than all she ever takes away."

Now do not go to thinking that Hester Bryan was a great strapping Amazon, and looked like a female prize-fighter. She was tall, and she was strong, and she was graceful as the Venus of the Porta Portese, if by good luck you ever saw her.

And she was as good as pretty; and she was the queen of the whole town, because she was pretty and good, and so bright. She never set herself up as grander than the other girls, and all the other girls set her up as the queen of their love and worship.

And the boys? Oh, that was of course. But then there were no "pretenders," as the French say. All that was settled long ago—as long ago as when she wore a sun-bonnet, and walked barefoot to school. Horace would always be waiting for her at the Five Corners, with the largest and ripest raspberries, or with whatever other offering was in season. As long ago as when he made his first canoe, there would hang under her window, before breakfast, great bunches of the earliest pond-lilies. As soon as it would do for these young folks to go on sleigh-rides, it was in Horace's cutter that Hester always rode. And when Hester sang in the choir, she always stood at the right hand of the altos, and just across the passage stood Horace, at the left hand of the tenors. Not a young man in the village interfered with Horace's pre-emption there. But not a young man in the village who did not stand by Horace as loyally as the girls stood by Hester; and if he had needed to summon a working party to build a bridge across a slue, that Hester might walk dry-shod with a white slipper on, why, all the young men of the neighborhood would be there as soon as Horace wound his horn.

A nice girl at the West once wrote me to ask why all the good young men, who were bright and spirited and nice, were in my books, and why, in fact, the bright boys, who knew something and could do something and could be something—in short, were agreeable—were apt to be lounging round liquor saloons in the village when they should be better employed. I told her, of course, to wait a little; that she was looking through some very small key-hole. How I wish that my unknown correspondent could have seen Horace Ray! He was handsome, he was bright, he was strong, he was steady, he was full of fun; he could read French well, and could talk German, and he knew enough Latin. And yet he did not lounge round a liquor saloon, and the minister was glad, and not sorry, that he sung in the choir.

When this story begins, Horace Ray was twenty-two years old, and Hester Bryan was twenty-one. I know that that is dreadfully old for a story, but how can I help that? Do you suppose I make it up as I go along? If they did not choose to be married when he was eighteen and she seventeen, can I help that? The truth is, that Hester's father was a man who liked to have his own way, and in some things had it. He had not had it in making a large fortune, though he had always tried for that. In that business he had failed,—had failed badly. He was always just close to it; but always, just as he touched the log on which he was to stand erect, quite out of the water, the log was pushed away by his touch, and floated quite out of reach, he paddling far behind. Hester's mother was in heaven, or things might have been made easier for her. As it was, her father would not hear of her marrying Horace till Horace should have something better than expectations, till he was fixed in a regular business, with a regular income. Perhaps Ohio is now so far established as a conservative and old-fashioned country that most fathers of charming girls in Ohio will agree with him. Yet I never heard of any one's starving in Ohio. They do say that no one was ever hungry there!

Because of this horrible sentence of old Mr. Bryan—because of this—the happiest day of Horace's life was the day when he could come, at last, to Hester, and could tell her that he was appointed assistant engineer on the Scioto Valley Railroad, with a salary of one thousand dollars a year, to be increased by one hundred dollars at the end of the first year. Here was the "regular income in the regular business," and now all would be well. Would she be married in church, or would she rather go to Columbus, to be married quietly? For his part, he was all ready; he would like to be married that day.

Of course this last part was only his little joke. But Hester, dear child, how well I remember how pretty and how cheerful she seemed all that week, and how little any of us thought of what was to come! Hester was by no means a prude, and she was as happy as he. And the news lighted up all the village.

Everybody knew it, from the canal-locks up to the mills, and everybody was glad. Horace Ray had a good place, and he and Hester Bryan could be married right away.

Four days that happy dream lasted; and even now Horace looks back on those four dream-days as days of unutterable joy and blessedness. He has a little portfolio which Hester herself made for him, and on the back of which she painted his own monogram. It lies among his choicest treasures, and is never handled but with the most dainty care. It contains every note she wrote him—five in all—as those blessed days went by. Them it contains—ah, the pity!—four little sunny songs which Horace wrote to her on four of those evenings, and which he sent to her on the four mornings, with the bunch of flowers which she found at the front-door as she threw it open. These the poor girl had to give back to him. And all this is tied with a bit of ribbon, which is stained yet by the moisture on the stems of the flowers it tied together,—a little bunch of roses which Hester gave to him. For, as you must hear, these four days came to an end.

Old Mr. Bryan came home—"old" he was called, in the fresh and active phrase of a young community, because he was older than John Bryan the miller.

In truth, our Mr. Bryan was forty-five. He came home—from no one knew where. He was in low spirits: that all men saw as he left the railroad station—the dépôt, as they called it. The boy who drove him to his home—that is, who drove the horse which dragged the wagon in which old Bryan was carried to his home—this boy, I say, did not dare allude to Horace's good news. Pretty Hester came running to meet him at the gate, fresh as a rose and glad as a sunbeam; but she saw that all was wrong. All the same, everything was pleasant and cheerful; the children were neat and nice in their best clothes, the supper was perfect, and no returning conqueror had ever a more happy welcome.

Before they slept, even to her downcast, not to say cross, father, Hester told her story,—her story and Horace's. But old Bryan took it very hardly. It was all nonsense, he said. She must not think of weddings. His was no house to be married from. He was ruined: those infernal Swartwouts and Dousterswivels, or whatever else may have been the names of the swindlers who had fooled him, had cleaned him out; and the sooner the town knew he was ruined, and the world, why, the better, he supposed. Poor old Bryan was really to be pitied this time. Often as he had fallen, he had never fallen so far; and it certainly seemed as if he had fallen into mud and slime so thick and so deep, in a bog so utterly without bottom, that for him there was no recovery.

"No time to talk of weddings." This was all old Bryan would say.

When Horace came to plead, it was no better. There was a time when old Bryan had liked Horace. If any man knew how to manage him, it was Horace. But now he was simply unmanageable, and too soon the reason appeared.

There was a St. Louis merchant whom Bryan had met at Columbus the winter when he represented the district in the Legislature. From the first they seemed to have been great friends. When our pretty Hester made her winter visit to Columbus, to stay with Mrs. Dunn, this de Alcantara saw her,—the Duke de Alcantara, the Columbus girls called him, mostly in joke, but partly in mystery; for it was whispered that he might be a duke in Spain if he chose to be. This was certain,—that he was very rich—very. Those who disliked him most—and some people disliked him very much—had to own that he was very rich. Black-haired he was, very dark of complexion, and, Horace said, and all the party of haters, odious in expression. But whether Horace would have said that, had the two not crossed each other's lines, who shall say? The truth is that Baltasar de Alcantara was a great diamond merchant.

And now the mystery appeared. Old Bryan said he could not talk of weddings, but soon enough he began to talk of one. Baltasar de Alcantara wanted to marry our Hester. This she had guessed at; but she had thought she had put a very summary end to it. She had said to him squarely, the last time she saw him, "Do you not know that I am engaged to be married, Mr. de Alcantara?" She had supposed that would be enough. She had not thought of the Oriental fashion of buying your wife; but Baltasar de Alcantara had. There must have been Eastern blood in him. Horace Ray, after he heard of the new proposal of marriage, said his rival had a nose which looked Eastern,— arched, but not Roman. However it was about the nose, the diamond merchant offered to buy our Hester. If she would marry him, or if old Bryan would make her marry him, he would lend old Bryan all the money he wanted, up to fifty thousand dollars, on his personal security; he would take at their face all old Bryan's worthless stock in the Green Bay Iron Company, and he would make old Bryan vice-president in the Cattaraugus and Tallahassee Railroad, of which he was a managing director. All this statement old Bryan repeated to our Hester.

Of course Hester refused point-blank. And then for six months—nay, ten— came awful times for her. Hard times had she seen in that house before, but nothing like these! Horace was banished first. She had to send back her engagement ring, and the letters and the songs I told you of. She had to promise not to meet him in the village, and she kept her promise; not to speak to him if she did meet him there. Then she could not go out anywhere. Then she was kept on bread and water, and the children too. Then there was this and that piece of furniture carried off to be sold at auction,—everything that was her mother's and that her mother prized. Then poor Hester fell sick, and almost died. As soon as she rallied at all, old Bryan began again. And then Hester capitulated. That horrid Duke de Alcantara came—he came after dark, and came in his own carriage all the way from the station at London. Our boys would have mobbed him, I believe. He came, and I am bound to say he behaved very well. He was not obtrusive. He was gentle and gentlemanly. And when he went away he put a ring on Hester's finger; and she did not throw it in his face, nor did she tear out his eyes.

And so it was settled. And the house was furnished again, and Betsey Boll and old Miss Tucker came back to work in the kitchen again, and old Bryan's bank account was better than it ever was. And on the 2d of April he went to Cincinnati to sit as V. P. of the C. and T. R. R. Co., and to draw his first quarter's salary.

And poor Horace never set his eyes on poor Hester's pale face.

And all the village knew that on the 15th of May Hester Bryan was to be married to the Duke de Alcantara. And Lucy Lander surrendered so far from the general tone of opinion of the girls as to agree to be a bridemaid. She had a splendid dress sent to her from St. Louis. Jane Forsyth and the other girls said they would burn at the stake first. But Lucy said—and I think she was right—that Hester had a right to have one friend near her to the last.

The wedding was to be at St. Louis at St. Jude's Church. The boys said it was Judas Iscariot's Church, but this was their mistake. They said the Duke de Alcantara was afraid to be married in Hester's home. This, I think, is probable. The arrangements were left mostly to "the Duke" and to old Bryan's sister, Mrs. Goole—a skinny, wiry, disagreeable person, of a very uncertain age, who had made herself so unpleasant to all the neighbors on her visit to her brother, many years ago, that she had never come again till now. Now that he needed some womenfolk, Mrs. Goole was summoned to the rescue.

CHAPTER II.

SOLD.

On the 14th of May, the Pullman palace, Cleopatra, was waiting on a sidetrack at London, ready to take its first trip. It had been chartered, John the porter said, by a chap from St. Louis, who was going to take quite a party there. A bridal party it was. How large the party was to be, the porter did not know, though it was important enough to him. But he had dusted the new plush, clean as it was, and had wiped off the wood-work, though he could not stain his cloth on it.

Presently the party came, headed by a dark gentleman talking to the station-master. The station-master introduced him to the conductor as Mr. De Alcantara. The eagle eye of the porter saw that there were twelve in the party. He waited for no introduction, but seized the hand-baggage and distributed it to the different sections. Meanwhile the party entered the car.

But though the porter had assigned to each of their grandeurs a section of four seats, they did not mount each a separate throne. On the contrary, a pleasant-looking young lady, who might perhaps be the bride, and two children, sat down in the middle of the car. The rest were distributed according to their different degrees of lack of acquaintanceship.

"I want to bid you good-by now, dears," said the bride to the children. "You see there'll be a great row when you go to bed, and to-morrow morning I'll have hardly time to kiss you. So while they're setting supper ready, and he's talking to papa, I'll tell you each one of my old stories—no, you're so old now, Edward, that I'll tell Amelia two stories, and you can listen if you want to. Then we'll have just as good a good-by as if it were to-morrow, and two—no, three sets of kisses."

"But it's not so very far to St. Louis—so far as to make much of a fuss about; and we'll come and see you, sha'n't we?" said Edward stoutly.

"Yes, if I stay in St. Louis all the time;" and the poor girl told how often she would have to go down the river, and sometimes even across the ocean to Amsterdam. But presently she began on her stories, and the children at least were happy till they were all called to supper.

And then, to the surprise of the porter, the splendid Mr. De Alcantara took out a dried-up little woman whom he had hardly noticed, while Mr. Bryan and the bride filled up the table.

And such a supper as it was! Though it was past eight, the cook gave them as solid a first course as his French education would allow him before he covered the little tables with salads and ices.

To old Bryan's surprise, Hester took a little of De Alcantara's champagne—not as much as her cousins behind her; but he had never known her to take wine even in his flush times. Not that he cared,—he saw two full bottles opposite,—but yet he noticed it. Perhaps it was that which gave her rosier cheeks than she had had for a month; and perhaps it was that which put her in such good spirits.

"I am quite relieved," said she, as the last waiter went out. "I really expected to see a wedding-cake come on after this luxury, and hear that Mr. Prayerbook was in the next car, ready to marry me or bury me."

"If I had known you expected it," said De Alcantara, "I should have had it ready. And even now, I dare say, there is a priest on the train, my dear."

"Oh no, indeed," said Mrs. Goole, who took everything in earnest; "it will be far better for you to retire now with the children. It's nine o'clock, and just think how hard a day you'll have to-morrow."

"I don't know," said Hester. "I think that it is never so hard to do a thing as to make up one's mind to it; and as for going to bed, I don't care to. Perhaps Mr. De Alcantara has a pack of cards or so with him, and then you can have some whist, aunt, and we— Shall we have Sancho Pedro or euchre, your Grace?"

"Grace me no grace," said De Alcantara, as cards were produced—to his credit, be it said, from a friend's portmanteau. "I vote for euchre, if it be for four hands; Pedro by itself is far from exciting."

"Not when it's played for love, your Grace?" said Hester.

Who shall say how much the Don understood of the gambling terms of Great Britain? He stumbled and said, "Certainly, if you put it in that way."

But Hester would not, and so De Alcantara took the home-bridemaid, Lucy Lander, as his partner, and a "son of St. Louis" sat opposite Hester.

"I didn't quite know what to think," said Lucy Lander, afterward, to her sister. "Sometimes I thought she had made up her mind to it, and then again I thought something awful would happen. You see, he kept calling her 'my dear,' and she never blushed nor anything, except once, when she was leaning back, shading her face with her cards, and then her eyes sort of glittered; it could hardly have been the light, you know. And once she had dealt, and the cards fell ace, two, three, four, and then Mr. Gardner, the St. Louis man, said, in a sort of hesitating way, 'That means kiss the dealer, you know'; and then the duke took up her hand, which was lying on the table, but she pulled it away, and said, 'Wait—till to-morrow.' That could have meant anything, you know."

And as Lucy sat and wondered, Hester sat and played, better than Lucy did, perhaps. She did not let De Alcantara kiss her hand, but she did laugh with him, and at him a little. She asked the St. Louis man if her hands were large enough to pass muster there, and then explained that her father took a Chicago paper. Indeed, so loud was the laughter of the gentlemen that Mrs. Goole kept looking round in an anxious way, and trying to catch Hester's eye. But Hester kept her back resolutely turned, and Lucy would not understand any telegrams from the chaperon; so when Mrs. Goole found, to her joy, that it was eleven, she broke up the somewhat shaky whist-table, and spoke to Hester.

"My dear," said she, "it is really too late for any one to stay up any longer. My girls must go, and you too."

So Hester jumped up, kissed her father good-night, and bade *au revoir* to De Alcantara. Then she turned to section six, directed by the obsequious John.

"Wait," said De Alcantara, "I have a surprise for you;" and he led her to number nine, where her immense Saratoga stood on the sofa. "If you need anything," said he, "you yourself have been careful that you will find it here." And he kissed his hand and walked forward. As Mr. Bryan was following, Mrs. Goole stopped him. Looking round to see that Hester had disappeared, she said,—

"Fergus, that girl of yours doesn't mean to be married to-morrow."

"How do you know that?" said old Bryan.

"I can see it; I've been watching her," said Mrs. Goole. "You see that you have the forward section; I have the rear one. She won't pass me in the night, whatever she does at your end."

"Do you mean to sit up all night?" said poor Bryan.

"Of course I do, fool!" said his tender sister, "and that you shall sit up all night, too. If you don't, there'll be no wedding to-morrow."

"Well," said Bryan, as his sister left him.

He thought it over with a cigar on the front platform, and decided that his sister was right. So he worked his way back to her section, and found her there, sitting on the edge of the berth, as grim as a sentinel at Pompeii.

"I'll do it," said he.

"You'd better," said she.

And so all night he sat on the edge of his berth and tried to read, and then took another cigar on the platform, and then back and forth, till his cigars were gone; but not a wink of sleep passed his eyes that night.

As for Mrs. Goole, who shall say what passed in her vigils? Certain she was that on that night no one passed her but the two conductors and one brakeman. She was once startled at Chimborazo as a new black face appeared; but it was explained that there was a change of porters, and whether Mungo or John it mattered little to her.

And so morning came. No, it is no business of mine to tell who slept and who did not; who dreamed, or what the dreams portended. Sunrise is sure, or well-nigh sure; and even in a sleeping-car morning comes. Mrs. Goole looked a little more scraggy and haggard than usual. The bridemaids did their best, in the way of toilet, in their somewhat limited dressing-room. Baltasar was radiant in a fresh paper collar,—the utmost that even wealth like his could produce, as one travelled forty miles an hour, on the morning of one's wedding-day. Mungo, the porter, "made up" the several sections one after another. From beds they became elegant sofas again, and only section six, Hester's section, was intact. Its heavy curtains hung as at midnight, secured half-way down, as one might see, by a heavy brooch which Baltasar himself had given her.

"Let her sleep," said Lucy Lander. "Perhaps she did not sleep well at first. I did not."

"Oh, yes," said Mrs. Goole grimly; "let her sleep. I never can sleep in these things. I sat up all night without a wink."

"Oh, yes, let her sleep," said her father; and so they dashed on. Eight o'clock passed, half-past eight, nine o'clock, and yet no sign from number six.

Meanwhile obsequious waiters came in from the kitchen-car. The breakfast would be spoiled,—one breakfast had been spoiled already. De Alcantara consulted with old Bryan.

"Lucy," said old Bryan at last to Lucy Lander, "you must wake her. You girls will faint without your coffee. And in half an hour more there will be no breakfast."

Lucy assented, a little unwillingly, went to number six, withdrew the brooch, and put her head inside the curtains, and then—a shriek from Lucy. She flung the curtains back, and no Hester was there!

What was worse, no Hester had been there. The compartment had not been "made up," it would seem. Here were the two sofas, here was the *Wreck of the Grosvenor*, here was a faded nosegay, just as they had left them when they fell to playing euchre. But here was no Hester Bryan. Where was the girl? What had she done with herself?

De Alcantara turned on Mrs. Goole like a wild creature. He was ready to throttle her in his rage. "This is some confounded joke of yours, ma'am!" But no; she was no such actress as to feign that dismay and horror.

"It is he," she shrieked, pointing at her speechless brother, "it is he! He fell asleep, and the minx passed him at his door."

No. Old Bryan was no such fool as to sleep at his post. "Sartin" he had not slept a wink since this porter came upon the train at Chimborazo. Porter and brakemen were alike confident that no one had left the car at either door. The brakemen testified for the whole time. The porter was certain after Chimborazo.

Then the window of number six was examined,—a double window, and stuck fast with new varnish. Everyone remembered that they could not start it the day before, when Hester tried to throw out a banana-peel. And if she had opened both windows, not Rebecca of York herself could have closed them after her, poised upon nothing, and the train rushing underneath at the rate of forty miles.

From section nine, however, which had not been made up, and of which the windows were ajar, Miriam Kuh, one of the St. Louis bridemaids, produced a handkerchief. It had lain on the top of the Saratoga trunk. It was Hester's handkerchief,—one of the *trousseau* handkerchiefs,—and tied in a close knot was the engagement-ring Baltasar de Alcantara had given her. Those windows —the windows of section nine—were ajar. But that proved nothing. Baltasar himself said he started those windows for more air after everyone was asleep. Besides, a hawk could not crowd out of those cracks; and if Hester had opened them further, how did she close them again?

All the same the porter and the brakemen were sure she had flung herself from number nine—most likely when they were crossing "the bridge." The brakeman offered confidentially to show any man for five dollars how it could be done.

Old Bryan was sure Mrs. Goole had slept on her post. Mrs. Goole was sure old Bryan had slept on his.

Baltasar de Alcantara was mad with rage, and the bridemaids were faint with hunger. Miss Kuh gave him the ring and handkerchief, and he flung both out of the open window.

The groomsmen stole forward into the kitchen and ate cold chops and flattened omelets. Some cold coffee was smuggled back to the bridemaids.

And so the express-train arrived at St. Louis, and the loafers at the station watched the arrival of the "special bridal-car," and no bride emerged therefrom! only some very sick bridemaids, some very cross groomsmen, a disgusted bridegroom, an angry father and a frightened aunt, and the gigantic Saratoga trunk.

"Where to?" asked the porters, who staggered under the trunk.

"Nowhere," answered De Alcantara, with a useless oath. "Leave it in your baggage-room till it is called for."

And he went his way.

CHAPTER III.

CAUGHT AND TOLD.

Yet there was a wedding after all! The sexton and organist at St. Jude's had not been summoned for nothing, nor the parsons. It was not in vain that Ax, Kidder, & Co. had spread a whole piece of Brussels carpet across the wide pavement of Eleventh Street, from the curb-stone up the church-steps into the very porch.

For, as Baltasar de Alcantara left the Central Station, just as he was stepping into the elegant coupé which awaited him, a wild, foreign-looking woman, with a little child in her arms, sprang across his way.

"Take your baby to your wedding," the wild creature cried, crazy with excitement.

Baltasar de Alcantara stopped a full minute without speech, looking at her. Then he laughed grimly. "Hold your jaw," he said. "You're just in time. You'll do. Stop your howling. Go dress yourself decently in a travelling dress, and be at the church at twelve,—not one minute late nor one minute early,—and, mind, a thick veil. Moses, go with her, and see that she is there."

And so he entered his coupé and rode to his hotel. And at noon his party passed up his aisle, and this Bohemian woman, led by Moses Gardner, walked up the other aisle. There was the least hitch in the service, as De Alcantara bade the minister substitute the name of Faris for Hester. But of the company assembled, not ten people knew that it was not the Ohio beauty who passed on De Alcantara's arm from the chancel to the vestry.

In the vestry, however, there was a different scene. Baltasar, black with rage, was still trying to be civil to the minister's clerk, whom he found there with a book, waiting for the bridegroom's signature. As he took the pen, from the side-door another gentleman entered, and, without giving the bridegroom time to write, said to him, "You will please come with me, sir."

"And who are you?" said De Alcantara, with another useless oath.

"You know me very well. I could have arrested you upstairs, but I am good-natured. I have the governor's warrant to deliver you to this gentleman, who arrived from London this morning. He represents the chief of police there. You are to answer in London for receiving Lady Eustace's diamonds. We have been waiting for you since Tuesday, but this gentleman only arrived this morning."

De Alcantara turned speechless upon the other, who, with the well-trained civility of an officer of high rank in the English police, hardly smiled. But the two recognized each other at a glance. De Alcantara had known the other long before. And even he felt that rage and oaths were useless.

"No," he said, as the other offered handcuffs; "*parole d'honneur.*" But the handcuffs were put on. And the officers declined his civil offer of his own coupé.

On the registry of St. Jude's Church there is one certificate which lacks the signature of the bridegroom and the bride.

In the state-prison at Amsterdam, prisoner No. 57, in Corridor D, is sentenced to hard labor for fourteen years. He is the Duke de Alcantara, without his mustache, and with very little of the rest of his hair. The London authorities gave him up to the Dutch, when they found that these last had the heaviest charges against him.

De Alcantara had known that the United States had no extradition treaty with Holland, but he had not rightly judged the ingenuity of the Dutch police.

Whoever else was at this wedding, old Bryan was not there, nor was Mrs. Goole. But thanks to the enterprise of the evening press of St. Louis, old Bryan learned, before five o'clock, where his son-in-law that was to be was spending his honeymoon. So did Mrs. Goole.

She waited on her brother to ask where she should go next. He bade her go home, and never let him see her face again. Nor did she, so far as I know.

For him, the poor "old" man—one can but pity him—took a return ticket to Blunt Axe, which is the station nearest to the bridge. There must be some watchman at the bridge, and perhaps he would know something. At the Central Station the obsequious Pullman's porter met him.

"Cleopatra, sir? Have your choice of berths, sir. Going home empty, sir."

So little did the porter remember the haggard man. Old Bryan did not reply. He shuffled by the porter. But the question reminded him of the Saratoga trunk, and after a moment's doubt he went to claim it.

"No, sir. Bring the check, sir. No baggage given here, sir, without the checks." Poor old man, he could even see the trunk. But the check, most likely, was in De Alcantara's pocket. He tried to explain.

"No use talking, sir. You keep this gentleman waiting. Bring the check." And all poor old Bryan could do was to select a seat in the car most distant from that fatal Cleopatra. The Pullman porter could enlist but three passengers for her,—Lucy Lander and the frightened Bryan children.

No! it was morning before they had any companions to whom to tell dreams or adventures. But, early in the morning, the train stops at Chimborazo. Poor old Bryan had left it in the night at Blunt Axe, and was even then scanning the rails of the fatal bridge and peering down into the river. Was this blood or iron-rust? Was yonder white gleam a bit of his child's clothing?

The train stops at Chimborazo. And Lucy Lander and the children are not to be longer alone. Horace Ray enters. Jane Forsyth enters. And here are Fanny and Alice and Emma—all the girls—and Walter and Siegfried and James—all the boys. We change porters. Here comes John, the boy we started with on the wedding journey.

Scree! Scree! "All aboard!" The train dashes away.

"John, you make up six," says Horace, to the amazement of all the others; and Horace stands by as John unbolts the upper berth and lets it down.

And there, as fresh as a rose, as if she were just waking from happy dreams—there lies, there smiles, our Hester! Yes, it is she. She rises on her elbow, she jumps into Horace's arms. Fairly before all these people—are they not friends, and true friends?—kisses her, and she kisses him.

"Did you sleep well, my darling?"

"I believe—well, I believe it has not seemed long. Yes, I must have slept sometimes."

And Horace slipped the old engagement-ring upon the naked finger.

"You may bring in breakfast, John."

And this time the breakfast was hot, the appetites were sure, and, without champagne, the party was merry.

Lucy Lander told the fate of Baltasar. Jane Foryth asked where the Saratoga trunk was, and Hester produced the check from her own pocket.

At the crossing at New Dutzow the Cleopatra was detached from the express-train, and, to the marvel of waiting Buckeye boys, passed up on the virgin rails of the Scioto Valley Line, unaccustomed to such wonders. A special engine was waiting. A short hour brought the merry party to Kiowa Centre. There was Horace's buggy, there were carriages galore, and a more modest procession than that of yesterday took them to the Methodist meeting-house.

And there Asbury Perham, who told me the end of the story, asked Horace Ray if he would have this woman to be his wedded wife. And he said, "I will."

And there the existence of Hester Bryan, my pretty friend, under that particular name which she had borne from her infancy, ended.

MAX KEESLER'S HORSE-CAR.

Yes, Mr. Keesler told me the story, virtually in confession. It is a queer story, and I was somewhat at loss as to the counsel I was to give him. So I take the gentle reader into my confidence and his. I may as well say, as I begin, that it was not in Boston or in Brooklyn or in New York that this happened. The place was a sea-board town, where most of the people lived in a pretty suburb, but came into the old compact city for their work and for their amusements.

CHAPTER I.

THE PAINT-SHOP.

"It all began with the paint-shop," he said.

I knew that "the dumb man's borders still increase," so I asked no question what the paint-shop was, and by listening I learned.

"The paint-shop was in the garden of the little house Bertha and I had hired just after Elaine was born. When the agent gave me the keys, he said, 'There is a paint-shop in the garden, but you can make that useful for something.'"

So, indeed, it proved. Max Keesler and Bertha Keesler did make the paint-shop good for something, as you shall see, if you dare keep on with the story. But he never thought of it at the beginning.

Max had married Bertha, prudently or imprudently, as you may think—prudently, I think—just because he loved her and she loved him. They were not quite penniless; they were not at all penniless. He had two or three thousand dollars in the savings-bank, and she had rather more in bonds. Max had a good berth, the day he was married, in a piano-forte factory. He earned his twenty-five dollars a week, with a good chance to earn more. I do not think they were imprudent at all.

But while they were on their wedding journey a panic began. Max always remembered afterward that he read of the first gust of misfortune in a Tribune which he bought in the train as they came from Niagara. That was the first gust, but by no means the last. The last? I should think not. Gusts, blasts, hurricanes, and typhoons came. Half the business establishments of the country went to the bottom of the oceans they were cruising on, and among the rest poor Max's own piano-forte factory. Nay, it seemed to Max that every other piano factory he ever heard of had gone under, or was likely to.

So that when the little Elaine was born, and they wanted to leave the boarding-house, which they hated, Max was out of work, and they were as economical as they could be. Still they determined that they would hire rooms somewhere, and keep house. Bertha knew she could manage better than that odious Mrs. Odonto, who polished their teeth so with her horrid steaks. And it ended in their hiring—dog-cheap, because times were so bad—this tumble-down old house on the corner of Madison Avenue and Sprigg Court, which, as you know, had a paint-shop in the garden.

"The truth is," said the agent, "that the Cosmopolitan Railway Company, when they began, hired the barn and fitted it up for a paint-shop. They would leave their cars there to dry. But that was long ago. And no one has wanted to hire these premises till now. You don't happen to know a painter you could underlet the shop to?"

No. Max knew no such painter. But he figured to himself better times, when they would fit up the paint-shop as a sort of summer music-room. And it was pleasant to know that they had something to let, if only any one wanted to hire.

All the same, as he said to me when he began his confession, all his guilt, if it were guilt, all the crime, where there was crime, was "along of the paint-shop," as the reader, if he be patient, shall see.

CHAPTER II.

THE WOMAN BEGAN IT.

"Did you ever notice," said Bertha, at tea one night, "that the rails still run into the paint-shop, just as when the railway people painted their cars there?"

"Why, of course I have," said Max, surprised. "They took up the frog in the avenue, but the old rails were not worth taking."

"I suppose so," said Bertha meekly. "I have been thinking," she said—"I have been wondering whether—don't you think we might—just while business is so dull, you know—have a car of our own?"

"Have a car of our own!" screamed Max, dropping knife and fork this time. "What do we want of a car?"

"We don't want it," said Bertha, "of course, unless other people want it." But then she went on to explain that, no matter how hard were the times, she observed that the street-cars were always full. People had to stand in them at night coming out from the theatre, although that did not seem right or fair. Bertha had measured the paint-shop, and had found that there was room enough in it not only for a car, but for two horses. The old loft of its early days, when it served for a stable, was left as it was made, big enough for a ton or two of hay. It had occurred to Bertha that, as Max had nothing else to do, he might buy two horses and a street-car, and earn a penny or two for Elaine's milk and oatmeal by running an opposition to the Cosmopolitan Company.

Max loved Bertha, and he greatly respected her judgment. But he was human, and therefore he pooh-poohed her plan as absurd—really because it was hers. All the same, after supper he went out and looked at the paint-shop; and the next morning he climbed into the loft and measured it. Poor Max, he had little enough else to do. He sawed and split all the wood. He made the fire. He would fain have cooked the dinner and set the table, but Bertha would not let him. He had nothing else to do. Not a piano-forte hammer was there to cover between the Penobscot and the Pacific, and the panic seemed more frightened and more frightful than ever. So Max did not waste any valuable time, though he did spend an hour in the old hay-loft.

And at dinner it was he who took up the subject.

"Who did you suppose would drive the horse-car, Bertha?"

"Why, I had thought you would. I knew you were on their list for a driver's place at the Cosmopolitan office. And I thought, if you had your own car, you could be your own driver."

"And who was to be conductor?"

Then Bertha shut the window, for fear the little birds should hear. And she said that it had made so much fun at Christmas when she dressed up in Floyd's ulster, and that even Max's father had not known her, that she had been thinking that if they only made evening trips, when it was dark, if Max always drove she should not be afraid to be conductor herself.

Oh, how Max screamed! He laughed, and he laughed, as if he had never laughed before. Then he stopped for a minute for breath, and then he laughed again. At first Bertha laughed, and then she was frightened, and then she was provoked.

"Why should I not be conductor? If you laugh any more, I shall offer myself to the company to-morrow, and I will wear a crimson satin frock, and a hat with an ostrich feather. Then we will see which car is the fullest. Cannot I hand a gentleman in quite as well as this assiduous squinting man who hands me in? Can't I make change as fast as that man who gave you a fifteen-cent bill for a quarter? I will not be laughed at, though I am a woman."

So Max stopped laughing for a minute. But he had laughed so much that they discussed no more details that day. Any allusion to fares or platforms or the rail was enough to make his face redden, and to compel him to crowd his handkerchief into his mouth. And Bertha would not encourage him by laughing when he did.

CHAPTER III.

A LODGMENT MADE.

All the same a lodgment had been made. The idea had been suggested to Max, and the little seed Bertha had planted did not die. Poor fellow! his name was on the lists of all the railway companies, and so were the names of five thousand other fellows out of work. His name was also on the postmaster's list of applicants for the next vacancy among clerks or carriers. The postmaster was amazingly civil; asked Max to write the name himself, so that there need be no mistake. So Max observed that his name came at the bottom of the seventh long column of K's, there being so many men whose name began with K who needed employment. He calculated roughly, from the size of the book, that about seven thousand men had applied before him. Then he went to the mayor to see if he could not be a policeman, or a messenger at the City Hall. He had first-rate introductions. The mayor's clerk was very civil, but he said that they had about eight thousand people waiting there. So Max's chances of serving the public seemed but poor.

And thus it was that he haunted the paint-shop more and more. At first he had no thought, of course, of anything so absurd as Bertha's plan; still, all the same, it would do no harm to think it over, and the thinking part he did, and he did it carefully and well. He went through all the experiences of driver and of conductor in his imagination. He made it his duty to ride on the front platform always as he went to town or returned, that he might catch the trick of the brakes, and be sure of the grades. Nay, he learned the price of cars, and found from what factories the Cosmopolitan was supplied.

When a man thus plans out a course of life, though he thinks he does it only for fun, it becomes all the more easy to step into it. If he has learned the part, he is much more likely to play it than he would be if he had it still to learn. And as times grew harder and harder, when at last Max had to make a second hole in his bank deposit, and a pretty large one too, tired with enforced idleness, as he had never been by cheerful work, Max took one of those steps which cannot be retraced. He wrote, what he used to call afterward "the fatal letter," on which all this story hangs.

But this was not till he had had a careful and loving talk with Bertha. He loved her more than ever, and he valued her more than ever, after this year and a half of married life. And Bertha could have said the like of Max. There was nothing she would not do for him, and she knew that there was nothing he would not do for her.

Max told her at last that he felt discouraged. Everybody said, "Go West": but what could he do at the West? He did not know how to plough, and she did not know how to make cheese. No. He said he had laughed at her plan of the street-car at first, but he believed there was "money in it." They would have to spend most of their little capital in the outfit. A span of horses and a car could not be had for nothing. But once bought, they were property. He did not think they had better try to run all day. That would tire Bertha, and the horses could not stand it. But if she were serious, he would try. He would write to Newcastle, to a firm of builders whom the Cosmopolitan had sometimes employed. He would look out for a span of horses and proper harness. If she would have her dress ready, they could at least try when the car arrived. If she did not like it, he would make some appeal to the builders to take the car off his hands. But, in short, he said, if she did not really, in her heart, favor the plan, he would never speak of it nor think of it again.

He was serious enough now. There was no laughing nor treating poor Bertha's plan as a joke. And she replied as seriously. They had always wished, she said, that his work was what she could help in. Here seemed to be a way to earn money, and, for that matter, to serve mankind too, where they could work together. True, the custom had been to carry on this business by large companies. But she saw no reason why a man and his wife should not carry it on as well as forty thousand shareholders. If it took her away from the baby, it would be different. But if they only went out evenings, after the little girl had gone to sleep, why, she always slept soundly till her father and mother came to bed, and Bertha would feel quite brave about leaving her.

So, as I said, the lodgment was made. After this serious talk, Max wrote the fatal letter to the car-builders.

It was in these words:—

"351 MADISON AVENUE, April 1, 1875.

"DEAR SIR,—Can you furnish one more car, same pattern and style as the last furnished for the Cosmopolitan Company? The sooner the better. You will be expected to deliver on the Delaware Bay Line of steamers for this port, and forward invoice to this address.

"Respectfully yours,
"MAX KEESLER."

To which came an answer that fortunately they had on hand such a car as he described, and that as soon as the last coat of paint and lettering could be put on, it should be shipped. Max wrote by return mail to order the words "Madison Avenue Line" painted on each side, to direct that the color should be the same as that of the Madison Avenue Line, and he inclosed a banker's draft for the amount. Never had the Newcastle builders been better pleased with the promptness of the pay.

And everything happened, as Max told me afterward, to favor his plans. The *Richard Penn* steamer chose to arrive just before seven o'clock in the afternoon. Max was waiting at the pier with his span of horses. The car could be seen prominent in the deck cargo. The clerks and agents were only too glad to be rid of her at once. Quarter of an hour did not pass before some sturdy Irishmen had run her upon the branch-rails which went down the pier. The horses behaved better than he dared expect. When he brought his new treasure in triumph into the paint-shop, and found Bertha, eager with excitement, waiting for him there, he told her that he had rejected, he believed, a hundred passengers by screaming, "Next car—next car!" as he had driven up through the city into the more sequestered avenue.

It was too late to go back, had they doubted.

But they did not doubt.

CHAPTER IV.

AN EXPERIMENT.

Bertha heard with delight, listened eagerly, and sympathized heartily. When Max had told his tale, he went round to his handsome span of horses to take off their collars and headstalls.

"Stop a minute, Max," said Bertha, who held his lantern; "stop a minute,—if you are not too tired. We shall do nothing else to-night. Suppose we just try one trip,—just for fun."

"But you are not ready."

"I? I will be ready as soon as you are. See!" and she vanished into the harness-room. Max hardly believed her; but he did unfasten his horses, a little clumsily, led them round to the other end of the car, and hooked on the heavy cross-bar; ran open the sliding-door of the shop, and looked out upon the stars; went to the back platform and loosened the brake there; and then, as he stepped down, he met a spruce, wide-awake young fellow, who said, "Hurry up, driver! Time's up; can't wait all night here."

"Bertha, my child," cried Max, "your own mother would not know you!"

"As to that, we'll see," said the young man. "All aboard!" and she struck the bell above her head with the most knowing air.

The trouble was, as Max said afterward, to run the wheels into the street-rails when no one was passing. But he had, with a good deal of care, wedged in some bits of iron, which made an inclined plane on the outside of the outer rail, and as the car was always light when he started, the horses and he together soon caught the knack. A minute, and they were free of the road, bowling along at the regulation pace of seven miles an hour. For their trip down and back they were quite free from official criticism. The office was at the upper end of Madison Avenue, a mile or more above them.

And never did young lover by the side of his mistress drive his span of bays through Central Park with more delight than Max drove Bertha in that glad minute when she stood on the platform by his side, before they were hailed by their first passenger.

Bertha will remember that old woman to her dying day,—an old Irishwoman, who, as Bertha believes, kept a boarding-house. She had with her an immense basket, redolent of cabbage, and of who shall say what else. No professional conductor would have let her carry that hundredweight of freight without an extra fare. But Bertha was so frightened as she asked for one fare that she had no thought of claiming two. Bertha made a pretext of helping the woman with the basket, knowing, as she did so, that it would have anchored her to the roadway had she been left alone with it. When basket and owner were well inside the car, Bertha put her head into the doorway, and said, as gruffly as she knew how, "You must put that basket with the driver if you expect us to take it." The poor woman was used to being bullied more severely, and meekly obeyed.

Next three giggling girls with two admirers, glorious in white satin neckties, all on their way to the Gayety, all talking together with their highkeyed voices, and each of the three determined not to be the one neglected in the attentions of the two. Great frolic, laughter, screaming on the high key, and rushing back and forward, before they determined whether they would sit all on one side, or three on one seat and two on the other, and in the latter case, which girl should be the third. Riot and screaming not much silenced by the entrance of three old gentlemen, also in white neckties, on their way to the Thursday Club. Two paper-hangers, late from an extra job, have to place their pails on the front platform, and stand there with their long boards. Next comes a frightened shop-girl from the country. It is her first experiment in going down to the city at night, and long ago she wished she had not tried it. But Bertha hands her in so pleasantly, and insists on making a seat for her so bravely that the poor, pale thing looks all gratitude as she cuddles back in the corner and makes herself as small as she can.

And at last there are so many that poor Bertha must force herself to go through the car and take up the fares. Nor is it so hard as it seemed. Some give unconsciously. Some are surprised, and dig out the money from deep recesses, as if it were an outrage that they should be expected to pay. One old gentleman even demands change for five dollars. But Bertha was all ready for that. She is more ready for the hard exigencies than she is for the easy ones. And when she comes to the front platform she taps the two paper-hangers quite bravely, and has quite a gruff voice as she bids Max to be sure and stop at the South Kensington crossing before they come to the gutter.

By and by, as they come nearer the city proper, the car and platforms fill up. Bertha pushes through on her second and third tour of collection, and at last, at a stop, runs forward to her husband. "Be sure you stop at Highgate. I shall be inside. But all these theatre people leave there." This aloud, and then she leaned down to whisper, "There are three men smoking on the platform, and they make me sick. What can I do?"

"I should like to thrash them," said Max, in a rage. "But you must bully them yourself. I'll stand by you, and will call an officer if there is a row."

Bertha gained new life, worked steadily back through the crowded passage, opened the door, and spoke:—

"Smoking not permitted, gentlemen. Lady faint inside."

Without a whisper the three men emptied their pipes and pocketed them, and Bertha had won her first great victory. The second never costs so much as the first, nor is it ever so remembered.

"Could you know—should you know—can you tell—about when we come to 97 Van Tromp Street, and would you kindly stop there?" This was the entreating request of the poor, frightened shop-girl.

"Certainly, ma'am; you said 97?" said Bertha, as grimly as before to the boarding-house keeper, but determined that that girl should go right, even if the car stopped an hour.

And when they came to 97, Bertha handed her down, and led her to the door, and pealed at the bell as if she had been a princess. "Oh, I thank you so!" said the poor, shrinking girl. "And please tell me when your car goes back. I will be all ready."

This, as Bertha says to this hour, was the greatest compliment of her life.

They came home light, for it was in that dead hour before the theatres and concerts are pouring out their thousands. Bertha did not forget 97 Van Tromp Street, and her poor little ewe-lamb was waiting at the door as the great car stopped itself, uncalled. As they approached Sprigg Court there was but one passenger left,—a poor tired newspaper man, going out to Station 11 to see who had cut his throat in that precinct, or what child had been run over.

"Far as we go," said Bertha, in her gruffest voice.

And the poor fellow, who was asleep, tumbled out, not knowing where he was, and unable, of course, to express his surprise.

CHAPTER V.

REGULAR WORK.

When they were once home, both of them were too much excited and quite too tired to think of a second round trip, even to catch the theatres. Glad enough were they to shut the paint-shop. Bertha held the lantern while Max rubbed down the horses and put them up for the night. Then she disappeared in the harness-room, re-appeared in her own character in a time incredibly short, and ran into the house at once to see how the baby was.

Baby! Dear little chit, she had not moved a hand since her mother left her. So, with a light heart, Bertha joined her husband in the kitchen.

They counted up the money, and subtracted what Bertha had started with. Happily for them, the Cosmopolitan had not then introduced the bell-punch, nor did it ever, so far as I know, introduce the bother of tickets. Max and Bertha followed in all regards the customs of the Cosmopolitan. The freight down town had been very large, the freight up had been light; but they were seven dollars and fifty-five cents richer than they were three hours before.

"How much money it looks like!" said Bertha. "Even with that old man's five-dollar bill, it makes so big a pile. I never saw two dollars in nickels before."

"I hope you may see a great many before you are done, my sweet," said Max cheerily.

"But is it fairly ours? Are you troubled about that?"

"I am sure we have worked for it," said Max, laughing. "I know I never worked so hard in my life, and I do not believe you ever did."

"No: if that were all."

"And is it not all? The car is bought with your money. The horses and their hay were bought with mine."

"But the rails," persisted Bertha, a little unfairly, as she had planned the whole.

"The rails," said Max coolly, "belong to the public. They are a part of the pavement of the street, as has been determined again and again. If I chose to have a coach built to run in the track, nobody could hinder me. This is my hackney-coach, and you and I are friends of the people."

So Bertha's conscience was appeased, and they went happily to bed.

The next morning Max came home in great glee. He had seen Mr. Federshall, his old foreman, who always was cordial and sympathetic. He had told Mr. Federshall where he lived; that he had an old stable on the premises, and that, for a little, he was keeping a pair of horses there; that he had no other regular employment. And Mr. Federshall, of his own accord, had asked him to keep his covered buggy. "I have had to sell my horses long ago," he said, laughing. And Max was to store the buggy, and take his pay in the use of it for nothing.

So they might go to ride that living morning with the span, take the baby, and have no end of a "good time."

A lovely day, and a lovely ride they had of it. The baby chirruped, and was delighted, and pretended to know cows when they were pointed out to her, as if, in fact, the poor wretch knew a cow from a smoke-stack. All the same, they enjoyed their new toy—and freedom.

With this bright omen "regular work" began. But they soon found that as "regular work" meant two round trips every evening, they must not often take the horses out in the morning. As Max pointed out to Bertha, they had better hire a horse for three dollars and a half than lose one round trip. So, in the long run, they only treated themselves to a drive on a birthday or other anniversary.

A good deal of the work was a mere dragging grind, as is true of most work. Bertha declared that it came by streaks. Some nights the passengers were all crazy: women would stop the car when they did not want to get out; people would come rushing down side-streets to come on board, who found they wanted to be put out as soon as they had entered; a sweet-faced little woman would discover, after she was well in, that she was going into town when she should be going out; another would make a great row, and declare she had paid a fare, and afterward find that she had it in her glove. And all these things would happen on the same night. On another night everything would be serene, and the people as regular as if they were checker-men or other puppets. They would sit where they ought, stand where they should, enter at the right place, leave where they meant to; and Bertha would have as little need to bother herself about them as about that dear little baby who was sleeping at home so sweetly.

The night which she now looks back upon with most terror, perhaps, was the night when a director of the Cosmopolitan came on board. She was frightened almost beyond words when the tidy old gentleman nodded and smiled with a patronizing air. Did he mean to insult her? She just turned to the passenger opposite, and then, with her utmost courage, she turned to him, and said firmly, "Fare sir."

"Fare? Why, my man, I am a director. I am Mr. Siebenhold."

The passengers all grinned, as if to say not to know Mr. Siebenhold was to argue one's self unknown. Bertha had to collect all her powers. What would the stiffest martinet do in her place? She gulped down her terror.

"I can't help that, sir. If you are a director, you have a director's pass, I suppose?"

Magnificent instinct of a woman! For Bertha had never heard of a director's pass nor contemplated the exigency.

"Pass?" said the great man. "Well, yes—pass? I suppose I have." And from the depths of an inside pocket a gigantic pocket-book appeared. From its depths, with just the least unnecessary display of greenbacks, a printed envelope appeared. From its depths a pink ticket, large and clean, appeared. "How will that do, my man?"

For all Bertha could see, the pass might have been in Sanskrit. Her eyes, indeed, were beginning to brim over. But she walked to the light, looked at the pass, said "All right" as she gave it back, and took out her own note-book to enter the free passenger.

"You've not been long on the line?" said the old gentleman fussily.

"Not very long, sir."

"Well, my lad"—more fussily—"you have done perfectly right—perfectly. I hope all the conductors are as careful. I shall name you to Mr. Beal. What is your number?"

Bertha pointed to her jaunty cap, and said "537" at the same moment. The old gentleman took down the number, and did not forget his promise.

The next day he talked to the superintendent an hour, to that worthy's great disgust. When Mr. Siebenhold left the office at last, the superintendent said to the cashier, "The old fool wanted 'to recommend No. 537.' I did not tell him that we only have three hundred and thirty men."

So Bertha passed her worst trial, as she thought it then. But a harder test was in store.

CHAPTER VI.

YOUR UNCLE.

The baby was growing to be no baby. She was big enough to run about the floor, and if they had a boiled chicken for dinner, the little girl sucked and even gnawed at the bones. The autumn had gone, and Bertha had a long winter ulster to do her cold work in, and Max a longer and a heavier one for his. Still, neither of them flinched. Max did not like his work as well as he liked covering piano-forte hammers, but he liked it better than nothing. And Bertha liked to be out of debt, and to see Max happy. So never did she ask him to drop a trip, and never did he ask her.

It was a light trip one evening, for the weather was disagreeable, and unless the theatre filled them up, it would be a very poor evening's work. As they went out of town nearly empty, Bertha came rushing out upon the front platform to Max, and said to him, in terror, "Your uncle and aunt are on board!"

"What?"

"Your Uncle Stephen, from New Britain, and your aunt, and they have two of your old-fashioned German carpet-bags, two baskets and a bird-cage. They are coming to make us a visit. He asked me very carefully to leave them at the corner of Sprigg Court."

"Make us a visit!" cried Max, aghast. "How can we run the car?"

"I don't know that," said Bertha. "I should like to know first how they are to get into the house."

"That, indeed," said Max; and, after a pause, "You must manage it somehow."

That is what men always say to their wives when the puzzle is beyond their own solution. And Bertha managed it. Fortunately for her, the night was dark. The old uncle and aunt were quite out of their latitude, and they didn't know their longitude. They were a good deal dazed by the unusual experience of travel. They were very obedient when Bertha stopped the car a full square before she came to her own house, and said,—

"You had better get out here. I will take your baskets and the cage." This she did, and deposited all three of the bipeds on the sidewalk. She bade them "Good evening" even, and, when the old gentleman had at last put his somewhat cumbrous question, "Could you kindly tell us on which corner Mr. Max Keesler lives?" the car was gone in the darkness.

Short work that night as Bertha doffed her ulster and assumed her home costume. For Max, he only tethered the horses, and then ran into the house, lighted it, and waited. Bertha joined him, however, before his uncle appeared. And leaving her in her own parlor, the guilty Max put on his hat, walked down the avenue, and met his dazed relatives, so that he could help them and the canary-bird and the baskets to his own door.

"Come, Bertha, come!" he cried. "Here is Uncle Stephen and my aunt!"

"Where did you drop from, dear aunt?" And the dear old lady explained how they had rung at the wrong door, how long the servant was in coming, and then how badly the servant understood their English.

"But how came you there at all?" persisted Bertha.

"Oh, the conductor left us at the wrong street."

"At the wrong street!" cried Bertha. "These conductors are so careless! But this man must have done it on purpose. What looking man was he?"

"My dear child," said her aunt, speaking in German, "you must not blame him; he was very young and very kind; perhaps he was a new man, and did not know. He was very kind, and carried the bird himself to the sidewalk."

After this, mischievous Mistress Bertha did not dare say a word.

But there was no second trip that evening.

Nor the next evening. Nor the next. Nor the next. Nor for many evenings more.

Max and Bertha took Uncle Stephen and their aunt to the little German play of the Turnverein; they took them to the German opera, which, by good luck, came to town, but they did not go in Max's car. Max took his aunt to ride one day, and another day he took Uncle Stephen, but not in his own car. The horses were eating their heads off, as he confessed to Bertha, but not a wisp of hay nor a grain of oats could he or she earn for them. One is glad to have his aunt and uncle come and see him. But how shall the pot boil if aunt and uncle cut off the channel through which the water flows to the pot, nay, block the wheels of the dray which brings the coal to the fire?

At last one fatal day Uncle Stephen, as he smoked his pipe, came out, as he was fond of doing, to the paint-shop to see Max rub down his horses. Nay, the old man walked out into the garden, threw out the lighted *Tabak* which he loved so well, threw off his coat, and with a wisp of straw rubbed down one horse himself.

"I show you how," he said. "The poor brute—you do not half groom him." This in German.

"Ah me!" Max replied. "We must groom them well. The proverb says, 'When the horse is to be sold, his skin must shine.'"

"Must he be sold, then, my boy?"

"Ah me! yes, he must be sold. He eats off his head. As the proverb says, 'If the man is hungry, the beast goes to the fair.'"

"Mein Gott!" said the old man, not irreverently; "it is indeed hard times."

"Hard times," said Max, "or I would not sell my bays. But the proverb says, 'It is better to go afoot fat than to be starved and ride.'"

"And what do these people pay you for storing this car here, my son?"

"Pay me? They pay not a pfennig. But the proverb says, 'Better fill your house with cats than leave it empty.'"

"Mein Gott! they should pay some rent," said the old man. "I see by the rail they use it sometimes."

And Max said nothing.

The next day the old man returned to the charge.

"My son Max," he said, "do this company keep their car here, and pay nothing?"

"They pay nothing," said Max. "The proverb says, 'The rich miller did not know that the mill-boy was hungry.'"

"My son Max, let us take out the car at night, and let us drive down town and back, and we will get some rent from them."

Guilty Max! He started as if he were shot.

"Max, my son, do you drive the horses, and I will be the boy behind—what you call conductor."

Guilty Max! His face was fire. He bent down and concealed himself behind the horse he was rubbing.

"What do you say, my son? Shall I not make as good conductor as my little Bertha?"

Then guilty Max knew that his uncle knew all. But indeed the old man had not suspected at the first. Only there had seemed to him something natural, which he could not understand, in the face of the handsome young conductor. But, as chance had ordered,—good luck, bad luck, let the reader say,—early the next morning, as he smoked his pipe before breakfast, he had walked into the paint-shop. Then he had stepped into the car. On the floor of the car he had found his wife's handkerchief, the loss of which she had deplored, and evident traces of birdseed from the cage. The old man was slow, but he was sure; and a few days of rapt meditation on these observations had brought him out on a result not far from true.

"My son," he said, after Max had made confession, "if the business is all right, as you say, why do we not follow it in the daytime?"

Max said that he did not like to expose Bertha to observation in the daytime.

"But, my son, why do you not expose me to observation in the daytime? If it is all right, I will go down town with you. I will go now."

Then Max said that, though it was all right according to the higher law, the local law had not yet been interpreted on this subject, and he was afraid the police would stop them.

"Ah, well, I understand," said the old man. "Let them stop us; let us have one grand lawsuit, and let us settle it forever."

Then Max explained, further, that he had no money for a lawsuit, and that before the suit was settled he should be penniless.

"Ah, well," said Uncle Stephen, "and I—who have money enough—I never yet spent a kreutzer at law, and, God willing, I never will. But, my son, let me tell you. What we do, let us do in the light. At night let us play, let us go to the theatre, let us dance, let us sing. If this business is good business, let us do it by daylight. Come with me. Let us see your bureau man—what you call him —Obermeister, surintendant. Come!" And he hauled guilty Max with him in a rival's car to the down-town office of Mr. Beal, the superintendent.

And then the End came.

CHAPTER VII.

THE END.

Max and his uncle entered the office, and were ushered into Mr. Beal's private room.

"Be seated, gentlemen—one moment;" and in a moment the tired man of affairs turned, with that uninterested bow, as if he knew they had nothing of any import to say.

But when Max, man fashion, held up his head and entered squarely on his story, Mr. Beal colored and was all attention. A minute more, and Mr. Beal rose and closed the door, that he might be sure they were not heard. Indeed, he listened eagerly, and yet as if he did not wish Max to be proved in the wrong.

"In short," said Max, at the end, "if what I have done is wrong, I have come to say that I do not want any fight with the company, and I should be glad to make amends."

Strange to say, the man of affairs hardly seemed to heed him. Mr. Beal was already in a brown study.

"Oh, yes, certainly. I am sure I am much obliged. I beg your pardon. Have you said all you wished to say?"

"Nothing more," said Max, half offended.

"I beg your pardon," said Mr. Beal again.

"I came to beg yours," said Max, just rising to the drollery of the position.

"I beg your pardon," said Mr. Beal once more, "but—I have been afraid—of this thing ever since I was on the line. You say you do not want to fight with the company. Quite right, young man, quite right! The company is friends with all the world, and wants no fighting."

But after this pacific beginning Mr. Beal went on to say that he was well aware, and that the directors were aware, that any man had a right to use their rails if he did not interfere with the public convenience. He did not say, but Max was quick enough to see, that the fact that he and Bertha had used the rails for so long a time, and the company never knew it, was itself evidence that the public had suffered no inconvenience.

In an instant Max saw, and his uncle saw, that Mr. Beal was much more anxious to keep this fact from the public than he was to apprehend any offenders, if offenders they had been.

"Mr. Keesler, the press would make no end of fun of us if this thing was known."

This after a pause.

"Suppose, Mr. Keesler, you turn your stock over to us, at a fair valuation, and I give you the first berth I have as a driver? I am afraid I cannot engage your conductor."

This with a sick smile. Max was amazed. He came to be scolded. It seemed he was expected to offer terms.

"Frankly, Mr. Keesler, we had rather not have much public discussion as to the rights of individuals to put their cars on our rails. You seem to be tired of the business. What do you say?"

Max made a very short answer.

The truth was, he was sick to death of the business. In very little time he had named his price for the car, and as soon as it was named, Mr. Beal agreed.

"But how shall I take possession?" said Mr. Beal. "If I send one of my men for it, the story will be in the Herald within three days."

"Trust me for that," said Max. "Till you have your car you need not send your check."

The Cosmopolitan cars do not run after midnight. At one the next morning Max drew out the fatal truck upon the avenue, down to the top of the steep grade at De Kalb Street, braked up, and then took off his horses. Then, with the exquisite relief with which a soldier after his enlistment leaves his barracks, Max loosened the brake, jumped from the platform, and saw the car run from him into the night.

The first morning driver on the Cosmopolitan, in the gray of the morning, met an empty car on the long causeway at Pitt's Dock. He coupled it to his own car, reported it, and was told to take it to the new Herkimer stables.

And   Max?

And Bertha?

Uncle Stephen and the good frau found life in Sprigg Court too comfortable to want to move. Little Elaine was such a pet, and dear Bertha was so much like her mother!

It ended when they took the rest of the house upstairs, and Uncle Stephen made Max his man of business in that curious commerce of his with Natal and the Mozambique Channel.

Still Max's conscience sometimes disturbs him. In one of such moods he comes to me to confess and receive counsel. Absolution I do not give.

And it is thus, gentle reader, that it happens that I tell his story to you.

THE MODERN PSYCHE.[1]

[1] Readers not quite at home in Mrs. Tighe or Apuleius may be glad to revive their memories of the ancient Psyche by this note from the Cyclopedia. The prettiest rendering of that story is in William Morris's "Earthly Paradise"; but the reader will ask himself seriously whether it be anything but an allegory to cover the moral in the matter-of-fact tale before him.

Psyche, whose two elder sisters were of moderate beauty, was so lovely that she was taken for Venus herself, and men dared only to adore her as a goddess, not to love her. This excited the jealousy of Venus, who, to revenge herself, ordered Cupid to inspire her with love for some contemptible wretch. But Cupid fell in love with her himself. Meanwhile her father, desiring to see his daughter married, consulted the oracle of Apollo, which commanded that Psyche should be conveyed, with funeral rites, to the summit of a mountain, and there left, for she was destined to be the bride of a destructive monster, in the form of a dragon, feared by gods and men. With sorrow was the oracle obeyed, and Psyche was left alone on the desert rock, when suddenly Zephyr hovers around her, gently raises and transports her to a beautiful palace of the God of Love, who visits her every night, unseen and unknown, leaving her at the approach of day. Perfect happiness would have been the lot of Psyche, if, obedient to the warning of her lover, she had never been curious to know him better. But by the artifices of her jealous sisters, whom she had admitted to visit her, contrary to the commands of Cupid, she was persuaded that she held a monster in her arms, and curiosity triumphed. As he slept, she entered with a lamp to examine him, and discovered the most beautiful of the gods. In her joy and astonishment she let a drop of the heated oil fall upon his shoulders. Cupid awoke, and, having reproached the astonished Psyche for her suspicions, fled. She wandered everywhere in search of her beloved, but she had lost him. Venus kept her near her person, treated her as a slave, and imposed on her the severest and most trying tasks. Psyche would have sunk under the burdens had not Cupid, who still tenderly loved her, secretly assisted her in her labors.

When Psyche was finally reunited to Cupid in Olympus, her envious sisters threw themselves from a precipice.

CHAPTER I.

No, I do not know by what accident it was that Edward Ross came to spend a week in August at the Columbia Hotel, at Hermon Springs.

No, and I do not know by what accident it was that all the Verneys were there. The home of the Verneys is at Painted Post, as I suppose you know. But this year the Verneys took a holiday for a month at the Columbia Hotel, and while they were away from home the ceilings were whitened, the house was painted inside and out, and new railings were added to the outside steps at the side door.

What I do know is that it was at the Columbia Hotel that Edward Ross first saw Psyche, who was the youngest daughter of the Verney household. All the world of the Columbia Hotel had gone across to the Solferino House, which was the other side of the way. There was a hop at the Solferino House, and the general public had gone to the hop. Ross had arrived late, the only passenger by that little one-horse railway from Hudson. He came into the great drawing-room, and thought he was alone. But he was not alone. Psyche, youngest of the Verney girls, was at the piano, not playing, but looking over some music which the Jeffrey girls had left there.

If you had asked the gossips of the hotel why Psyche did not go to the hop where all her older sisters had gone, you would have been told that she was but the half-sister of the other Verneys; that since her mother died, these three older sisters had held a hard rein on poor Psyche; that some one of them had laid down the law that there were so many of them they must not all go together to any frolic. In the interpretation of this law, Psyche always stayed at home if the party were pleasant, and one or two of the older sisters stayed if it were likely to be stupid. This is what the gossips of the hotel would have said, and this is what I believe.

Anyway, it happened that on this particular evening Edward Ross threw himself at length on a long sofa in the drawing-room, not knowing that any one was there; and little Psyche, not knowing that he had come in, crooned over the Jeffreys' music, and at last picked out something from Mercadante which she had never seen before, and which did not seem to her very difficult, and, after she had read the whole page down, tried it, and tried it again, in her resolute, wide-awake, very satisfactory way.

The third time she tried she was quite well pleased with her own success, and this time, as she came down to the last staff, upon that first page, Edward Ross's hand appeared on the top of the page, ready to turn it over. Psyche neither screamed nor flinched. She nodded simply: she was under the inspiration of the music now, and she played well. She played the whole piece through. Then he thanked her, and she thanked him. She played a good deal for him that evening. He brought down his William Morris and showed it to her, and read to her some of the best things in it. And so they spent two hours together very nicely, and by the time the madding crowd came back from the Solferino House, Psyche was not in the least sorry that she had not gone to the hop, and Edward Ross was very glad she had not gone.

There is a lovely little burn or brook which runs through a shady ravine behind the Columbia House, I forget what they call it. It might be called the Lovers' Brook or the Maiden's Home or the Fairy's Bath, or anything that verdant seventeen thought sweet enough. Age cannot wither nor custom stale its infinite variety. Edward Ross found no difficulty in making up a party of the young people at the hotel to go on a picnic up this brook the next day. By some device he made Agnes Verney think she would stay at home to flirt with an old West Indian, who was far too gouty to go even to the first fall. This left the pretty Psyche free to go. And she went, in the charming adornment of the unadorned simplicity of her pretty mountain walking-dress. And there were quite as many gentlemen as there were ladies, to help at all the hard fords and to lift them at all the steep climbings. So Priscilla Verney had her cavalier, and Polly Verney, whom the young men called "Bloody Mary," had her Philip, and the Garner girls were taken care of, and the Spragues and the Dunstables. For every girl, there was a young man; and if at most of the separating places Edward Ross and my pretty Psyche were together, it was not that they did not their full duty by society; for they did.

And a very pleasant day it was. That day Jabez Sprague asked Ann Garner to marry him, and she refused him point-blank: that made it a very pleasant day to her. That day Tunstall Dunstable asked Martha Jeffrey to marry him, and she said she would: that made it a very pleasant day to her. They all came home at five or six in the afternoon, very bright and jolly most of them, and those who were not bright and jolly pretended they were. Edward Ross had not asked Psyche to marry him, but I believe they had enjoyed the day as much as any one.

He had found out that this simple, shy, pretty little thing, who was snubbed in the household, who was left in the cold in their arrangements, and seemed to have no friends, had, all the same, a sweet, happy, contented temper; that she had her own notions and enthusiasms about books and men and duties; that she could not be made to say that yellow was white, or even that crimson was scarlet; that she never said she understood a thing but could not express herself, or that she knew a thing unless she did know it. He found a woman of principle under the form and method and semblance of a child.

And she had found out a man as fond of ferns as she was, who knew every fern in this glen, and every fern like it in the Himalayas; a man as fond of music as she was, who could not play as well as she could, and yet he had heard Chopin play, had seen "The Huguenots" in Paris, and had dined with

Lang and Bennett and the Abbé Liszt himself. This man loved her heroes, though he had travelled in a stage-coach with Wendell Phillips, and had helped Mr. Sumner look up the authorities for one of his speeches. This man could quote twenty lines of Tennyson to her one, he had met Christina Rossetti at a party; and yet he really deferred to Psyche's own recollection of a stanza of Mrs. Browning's which he had quoted wrong. Psyche was not used to men who dared show their enthusiasm, who dared confess their ignorance, who dared speak as if it were a matter of course to trust God's love, and who owned they had other objects in life than making money. Psyche and Edward Ross returned to the hotel after a very happy day.

The next day Edward Ross brought out the largest and best apparatus for water-color work that Psyche or any of the girls had ever seen. And before long it proved that, though one "had no talent for drawing," and another "could not sketch from nature," and another "could not do landscape," and another "hated trees," that on the broad piazza of the Columbia House five or six of them, Psyche included, could spend a very pleasant morning, under his directions, reproducing, after a fashion, on various blocks and in various books, the outlines of the blue Hoosac Mountains and of the valleys between. And my pretty Psyche went far beyond any of the rest, because she did as she was bid; she had no conceit about her own ways; she waited till her teacher could attend to her; she did not want to attract the attention of all the gentlemen on the piazza; and she was not gabbling all the time she was working. So that day they had a very happy day.

It is not within the space assigned to this story to tell how pleasantly the rainy morning passed when Edward Ross read the "Earthly Paradise" aloud to them, nor to describe the excursion which he organized to Williams College Commencement, nor the party which he made to see the Shakers, nor the evening concert of vocal and instrumental music which he arranged, and for which he had such funny bills printed at Pittsfield. No; these and the other triumphs of that week, long remembered, shall be unrecorded.

Of its history, this is all that shall be told: that on Saturday Edward Ross told Psyche that he loved her more than he loved his own life. She told him that she loved him more than she loved hers. And so it was that, in the exquisite joy of the new discovery of what life is and what it is for, Edward Ross accompanied the Verneys on their way home to Painted Post on Monday. There he asked for and there he gained the consent of Psyche's father for their speedy marriage.

On Tuesday he had to go home to Boston, for his holiday was over. It was a bitter parting, as you may imagine, between him and his Psyche, who had never been separated for more than ten hours at a time till now. For the last farewell Psyche took him on her favorite walk at Painted Post. It is only less beautiful than the "Vestal's Glade," or whatever we determined to call that burnie at Hermon.

"Dear Psyche," said he to her, "your life is mine henceforth, and mine is yours. God knows I have but one wish and one prayer henceforth, and those are to make you happy. It is because I wish that you may be happy that I ask one thing now. Do you think you can grant it? It is a very great thing to ask."

"Can I?" said the proud girl. "Why, darling, you do not know me yet." She had never called him "darling" till an hour before.

"You must not promise till you know," said Edward Ross.

"I can promise and I will promise now. There is nothing you think right to ask which I shall not think it right to do."

"Dearest, I do think this is right; I know it is right. It is because I know it, because we shall be ten thousand times happier, and because I shall be ten thousand times better for it, that I ask it. I would not dream of it but for your sake—" And he paused.

"Why do you stop, my dear Edward? I have promised. What shall I do?"

"Dearest, you are to do nothing. Simply, you are not to ask what my daily duty is, and you are not to ask me to introduce you to my friends. It separates me less from my sunbeam than most men's cares. Without knowing it, you can help me in a thousand ways in it. But to know what it is will only bring care on you and grief on me. Can we not live, as you trust me and as I love you, without my worrying you with these petty cares?"

"Is that all?" said Psyche, with her pretty laugh. "Why, darling, if it were to sweep the street-crossing,—as in that funny story you told us,—I would sweep too. If it were to keep a gambling-table, you would not have asked me to marry you. It is something honorable, that I know, because you are my own Edward. Why need I know anything more?"

And he kissed her, and she kissed him; and they went home to his little lunch; and then the express swept by, with Jim Fisk in uniform, as it happened, in a palace-car. And so Edward Ross went to Boston and made ready for his wedding.

CHAPTER II.

And a perfect wedding it was. I doubt if Painted Post remembers a prettier wedding or a prettier bride. And in that same express train Mr. E. Ross and his pretty bride swept off to New York, and so to Boston; and there he took her to the first sight of her pretty home.

How pretty it was! It was in Roxbury, so it was half country; and there was a pretty garden, with a little greenhouse such as Psyche had always longed for. Nay, there was even a fern-house, with just the ferns she loved, and with those other Himalaya ferns which he had talked of on that lovely first day of all. And there was a perfect grand piano, of a tone so sweet, and only one piece of music on the open rack, and that was the Mercadante of the first evening. And when they went upstairs, Psyche's own dressing-room was papered with the same paper which her pretty room had at her old home, and the carpet on the floor was the same, and every dear picture of her girlhood's collections was duplicated; and just where the cage of her pretty bullfinch, Tom, had hung, there hung just such a cage. Why, it was her cage, and her Tom was in it!

For Psyche and Edward had spent a night and a day in New York, that she might see Mr. Stewart's pictures and Mr. Johnson's; but Edward's office-boy, who had been left at Painted Post especially that he might bring the bullfinch, had taken a later train, indeed, but had come through without stopping.

And when they went into Edward's little den, it had but two pictures: one was Psyche's portrait, and the other was that miserable little first picture of the Hoosac Hills.

And then such a happy life began for these young people! No, Psyche did not find housekeeping hard. She had been the Cinderella at Mr. Verney's house too long for that. Now that she was the mistress of servants, she knew how to be kind to them and to enter into their lives. As Mrs. Wells says, "she tried the Golden Rule" with them. She loved them, and they loved her. And Edward was always devising ways to systematize the housekeeping and make it easier. Every morning he worked in his study for two hours, and she "stepped round" for an hour, and then lay on the lounge for an hour, reading by herself. Then he and she had two golden hours together. They made themselves boy and girl again. Two days in the week they painted with the water-colors; and Psyche really passed her master, for her eye for color was, oh! much better than his. Two days they worked at their music together—worked, not played. Two days they read together, he to her or she to him. And after lunch he always took his nap; and then, if it were cool enough, the horses came round, and he took Psyche off on one of the beautiful drives of Brookline or Milton or Newton or distant Needham; and she learned the road so well and learned to drive so well that she would take him as often as he took her. And at five they were at home, and at six Psyche's charming little dinner was served, always so perfectly; and then at eight o'clock he always kissed her, and said,

"Good-by, sweet; now I must go out a little while. Do not think of sitting up for me." And then Psyche wrote her letters home or read a while; and at ten she went to bed, and fell asleep, wondering how she could have lived before she was so happy.

And in the morning her husband was always asleep at her side. He slept so heavily that she would try to get up and dress without his knowing it. But he always did know. And because he could dress quicker than she, he would put on his heavy Persian dressing-robe, after he had plunged his head into cold water, and while she "did her hair" he would read her "Amadis of Gaul," or the "Arabian Nights," or "Ogier the Dane," or the "Tales of the Round Table," till he saw she was within five minutes of being done. Then he would put down the book—yes, though Oriana were screaming in the arms of a giant— and he would run and dress himself, and they would run a race to see which should first reach the piazza and give to the other the first morning-glory.

And then would come another happy day, like and yet unlike to yesterday.

No one called, you see. But I do not think Psyche cared for that. She always hated to make calls, nor did she want much to receive them. Both she and Edward were alone fully half their lives, though sometimes he would call her into the study to work with him, and often he would come to her to work with her. He would ask her if she was lonely, and he planned visits from his sisters, who were very nice girls, and his mother, who was perfectly lovely, and after a while, from some of the Western girls whom Psyche had known at the Ingham University. But never, by any accident, did any visitor come who made any allusion to his daily business. He never spoke of it to Psyche, and she, dear child, thought of it much less than you would think. She had promised not to ask, and she had sense to learn that the best way not to ask was not to care. Yes, Versatilla, dear,—and a girl of principle who determines not to care will not care. She knows how to will and to do.

I do not know whether Psyche the more enjoyed the opera or the pictures which she and Edward saw together. There seemed to her to be no nice private house in Boston where dear Edward did not seem welcome when he sent in his card, and asked if he and Mrs. Ross might see the pictures. Psyche often said that she owned more Corots and Calames, more Daubignys and Merles and Millets and Bonnats than any lady in the land, and that she kept them in more galleries. At the opera they often found pleasant people whom Edward knew sitting next to them, and they always chided him that he was such a stranger; and he always introduced Psyche to them as his wife as proudly as a king; and with many of these people she talked pleasantly, and some of them she met and bowed to at church or as they were driving. But none of them ever called upon her, nor did she call upon them. One day she said to Edward that she believed he knew more people than anybody else in the world. And he said, with a sad sigh, "I am afraid I do"; and she saw that it worried him, and so the dear child said no more.

In all this happy time Psyche had had no visit from her own sisters. Perhaps that was one reason why it was so happy. But it happened, after a happy life of a year and more, that a darling baby boy came to Psyche to make her wonder how she could have thought her life before was life at all. And the birth of the boy and his wonderful gifts were duly reported in the letters to Painted Post, and then there came quite a hard letter from Priscilla, putting in form the complaint that neither of the sisters had ever been asked to make Psyche a visit since they were married.

Psyche showed the letter to Edward on the moment, and he laughed.

"I have only wondered it did not come before."

Psyche tried to laugh too, but she came very near crying. "I have not wanted them to come before, and I don't want them to come now."

"Then they shall not come," said Edward, laughing again, and taking her on his knee.

"But I do want them to come, partly. I wish they had come and had gone, and that it was all over. It does not seem quite nice that my own sisters should not visit me."

"Well, my darling, as to that, they are not your own sisters; and even if Mrs. Grundy does not think it is quite nice, I do not know why you and I should care. Still, if you want to have them and have it over, let them come. '*Olim meminisse juvabit.*' That means, 'You will be glad to remember it.'"

Psyche said she knew that; and she pulled his whiskers for him because he pretended to think she did not; and he kissed her, and she kissed him. And so the next day, after Psyche had written ten different letters and had torn them up, she concocted the following, which, as it met Edward's approval, was despatched to Painted Post by the mail of the same evening:—

"Roxbury, May 10, 18—.

"My Dear Priscilla,—Indeed you must not think that Edward has prevented me from asking you to make a visit here. If it gives you any pleasure to come and see me and my housekeeping, you know very well how much pleasure it will give to me. You know we live very quietly, and are not in the least gay; so I think you must all come together and entertain each other. But little Geoffrey will entertain you, and you will think he is the dearest little fellow that ever lived.

"Come as soon as you can, for we are all going to the sea-shore on the 25th, and if you do not come soon it will be a very short visit."

141

And then the letter went on about Ann Garner's engagement, and the new styles for prints, and so on.

So the invitation was well over.

CHAPTER III.

If Edward Ross, or Psyche his wife, or Bim, the nurse of Geoffrey his son, had any hope that Agnes Verney and Priscilla Verney, and Bloody Mary, their sister, would decline the invitation, or that any one of them would decline it, they were very much mistaken. Allowing a day and a half for the letter to go to Painted Post, and a day for the three ladies to pack their trunks, and a day and a half for them to come to Boston, you have four days, which is precisely the interval which passed between the mailing of the letter and the arrival, late at night, of a carriage at Edward Ross's door with the three ladies, and of an express-wagon with the six trunks with which they had prepared for the ten days' visit. This was the night of the 14th, and, as they had been kindly informed by Psyche, their visit must end on the 24th.

And such a visit as it was! Not one day was unprovided for by Edward's forethought, and one amusement after another crowded upon the time, so that, if it were possible, the three ladies might not have a moment's time either for caballing against each other, or for lecturing poor Psyche. It was a little funny to see how, as a matter of course, they all taught her how to carry on her household. They would tell her, to Edward's great amusement and to her well-concealed rage, how to cheapen her mutton, how to keep her butter, how to save eggs in her sponge-cake, and even how to arrange the dishes on the table. Everything was elegant and tasteful in Psyche's house, wholly beyond any standard which they had ever seen at home; but all the same, they would make this suggestion and give that direction, as if, she said to her husband, crying, one morning—"as if this were poor papa's house, and I were Cinderella again."

And Edward only laughed and kissed her, and said, "O my sunbeam, keep a bright eye for them! There are now only six days more, and then Mrs. Grundy will be satisfied. '*Olim meminisse juvabit*.'" And then he pinched her ear, and she pulled his whiskers, and she laughed through her tears.

The first day was a day fresh from heaven; the apple-blossoms were in their prime, the air was sweetness itself; and after a late breakfast two pretty carriages came to the door. And Psyche took Agnes, who was the least hateful of the three, in her little pony-carriage, and herself drove Puss and Doll, her pretty ponies, after she had given to each an Albert biscuit from her own hand. And Edward took Priscilla and Bloody Mary with him, and as he passed the Norfolk House, he stopped and picked up Jerry Fordyce, who was stout and handsome and jolly, and Jerry took the back seat with Bloody Mary, and flirted desperately with her all that day, while Priscilla sat with Edward, and for miles on miles drove his beautiful bays. And they took a drive more lovely than any of these girls had ever seen. They came out upon the sea-shore—I will not tell you where. They ate such a dinner as neither Bloody Mary nor Agnes nor Priscilla had ever dreamed of. They came home by five in the afternoon, and Edward made all the women lie down and sleep. And when they had waked, he made them all dress again, and there were two carriages at the door, which took them to see Warren at the Museum. And they laughed till they almost died. And then they had a charming little supper in a private room at Copeland's; and after midnight they all came home. And this was what Psyche meant when she said she lived very quietly, and was not at all gay!

Bloody Mary was literary, and she had said at breakfast, the first day, that she hoped they should see some of the Boston *literati;* that she should be ashamed to go home to Painted Post unless she had seen Mr. Fields and Mr. Lowell and Mr. Longfellow and Dr. Holmes. And the second day, Edward said, should be Polly's day, and they should see the bookshops and the libraries. So this day he did not order the ponies, but two open barouches came up, and they drove first to the dear old corner of Hamilton Place, and went up to the pretty "authors' parlor" of Fields & Osgood. And Mr. Fields came in and told them some very pretty stories, and gave Bloody Mary an autograph of Tennyson; and Mr. Osgood and Mr. Clark came in and showed them the English advance-sheets of the new Trollope, and some copy of the new Dickens in manuscript. And the gentlemen begged all the ladies to come up whenever they passed in shopping. Then Edward took them to the Historical Rooms, and they saw Prescott's sword and Linzee's. Mr. Winthrop happened to come in, and they saw him; and Dr. Holmes was there, looking at some old MSS., and he was very courteous to the ladies, and showed Miss Polly the picture of Sebastian Cabot. Then they drove out to the College Library, and while they were looking at the old missals and evangelistaries, it happened that Mr. Longfellow crossed the hall and spoke to Edward; and Edward actually asked Agnes and Polly if he might present Mr. Longfellow to them; and then found Priscilla, and presented him to her and to Psyche. And when Mr. Longfellow found they were strangers, he told them just what they should see and how they should see it. And Polly slipped out her album, and he wrote his name in it, and said he was sorry he could not stay longer; but he pointed out to her some of the most interesting autographs there. And then they started for the

Museum, and by great good luck they met Lowell in Professors' Row. And Edward stopped the carriage, actually, and hailed him, and asked if he should be at home in an hour; and when Mr. Lowell said he was engaged with a class, Edward arranged—so promptly!—that they should all go and hear his lecture. And then they went to the Museum, and by the same wonderful luck Agassiz was going out as they came in; and he turned back, and showed the ladies everything. That was a day indeed! They came home to the most beautiful little family dinner, and in the evening they all went to Selwyn's Theatre, where was another charming play.

There was quite a similar day on the strength of a word from Agnes. Agnes was so much awed at first by Edward's hospitable condescension and by his giving up so much of his time to them that she did not dare to be cross for the first four days. But she did say to him that Polly's pretence of letters was all nonsense, and, that for her part, she was interested in politics and social reform; that at an era like that, when etc., etc., etc., every true woman ought etc., etc., etc., for the benefit of etc., etc., etc. So the very next day he showed them all a note from Mr. Sumner, saying that if the ladies would excuse the formality of a call, he should be happy to show them his prints and some other things which would please them at noon, and enclosing tickets for reserved seats to an address he was to deliver in the evening. That day was wholly given to politics and politicians. They went to the State-House, and sat in a sort of private gallery, when the young Duke of Gerolstein, who was on his travels, was received on the floor; and several very handsome and very nice young senators and representatives came up and were presented to the ladies. And when it came time for lunch, Edward invited three of the very nicest to go down to Parker's to a little dinner he had ordered there, and they had a very jolly time, in which Agnes studied social reform with a very merry senator from Essex County, quite to her heart's content.

As for Priscilla, she spoke but coldly of literature and politics, though she did not object to the dinner at Parker's or to flirting with senators. But she said to Edward that her heart was with the poor and sinful; that she would gladly do something in this complex civilization of ours to save those that were lost. How happy could she be if she were only eating locusts and wild honey on the brink of Jordan! But that seemed impossible, and she sighed. So a day was arranged for charity and its ministers—failing locusts. Fortunately the Diocesan Convention was in session, and among the presbyters and delegates Edward seemed as much at home and at ease as among the *literati* and the politicians. He presented Dr. Temple and Dr. South and Mr. Teinagle to the girls, and these gentlemen explained to them all the proceedings. At the little lunch for delegates and their wives, the bishop spoke courteously to all of them, and Edward brought to them the very famous Bishop of Parabata, who was on his travels to a Pan-Anglican Council. After the lunch they heard Mr. Tillotson preach, and then they were whisked down to the North End Mission, where there was that day an entertainment for destitute shop-girls. And here Mrs. Oberlin, a very famous philanthropist, enlisted them all to help her in her table at the great Fair in the Music Hall for the benefit of the mission; and then the next day all the girls spent a very charitable and very successful afternoon.

But I did not describe that week at Hermon. Why should I describe these ten days at Boston? A day at Nahant, *al fresco*, with two perfect black waiters, who arranged the lunch on the grass, because no one had moved down to Nahant so early; a visit to Plymouth and the Forefathers' Rock; a visit to the Antiquarian Hall at Worcester, and one to the witches' home at Salem,—these occupied so many days. Then there was the famous ball given by the City of Boston to the Duke of Gerolstein in the Boston Theatre, when all Colonnade Row was taken for supper-tables.

The old rules of the Verney family were wholly violated: all four of the girls went; and they danced with elegant young men till they almost died. And at last not only the ball was over, but everything else was over; and on the 24th of May the girls went home, after such a visit as even they were staggered to look back upon.

Edward and Psyche took them to the train, and, when it had fairly rolled out of the station, she took both his hands, and they looked each other in the face and laughed till the tears ran out of all four eyes. And, as they mounted the carriage, Psyche said, "Now we will live like civilized beings again!"

CHAPTER IV.

Dear Psyche, could you not cast the future better?

That day, as they had arranged, she packed her things and Geoffrey's for the country, and the next day they went, bag and baggage, to a beautiful place Mr. Ross had hired, at the corner of Hale Street and Beach Street, for a sea-shore home in Beverly, so that dear Geoffrey might have the south wind off the sea, the purest of air, and the freshest of salt-water brought up for his daily bath.

The only grief was that Edward had to take the evening train for Boston five nights in the week. But he always appeared fresh and bright at breakfast; and in the bath at noon, in the daily walk, or in the evening ride to the station, life seemed all the happier because the three hags of Painted Post had returned to their lair.

But this paradise lasted only a fortnight, when the tempter came. This letter arrived from Priscilla:—

"Very Private.

"PAINTED POST, June 5.

"MY DEAREST PSYCHE,—Your sisters and I have had a very serious *conversation* about you and the *life* you are leading. You seem to be very *happy;* but have you *thought*, my dear Psyche, that you are *dancing* on the edge of a volcano? Have you asked no *question* as to the future? Are you so blinded as *to forget* that the wages of sin is death, and that *the joys* of this moment are as nothing compared with *the terrors* of eternity?

"Your *sisters* and I have spoken to *dear papa* about the *life you lead*. He has *bidden* me write to you just what *I think*, and your sisters also say it is my *duty* to do so. I write you, *therefore*—how sadly you know—to say that, as a *Christian woman*, you *ought not to continue* in this life. You *should* rise above it, and assert the *freedom* of a child of God. *What is a dinner* at Parker's if eaten with a *guilty conscience?* Better is a dinner of herbs where love is.

"*I am sorry* to write you a *letter* which seems severe. But *you know*, my dear child, that I am as *a mother* to you. And *surely* the counsels of a mother will be *sweeter* to you than the *flatteries* of any not so near as she.

"Always your loving sister,
"PRISCILLA."

"Counsels of a fiddlestick!" said Psyche; and she wrote this answer:—

"What in the world is the matter? I saw no dislike of Parker's dinners when you were here. I believe you are crazy.

"Always yours,
"PSYCHE."

And she threw Priscilla's letter into the kitchen-fire. This was her mistake. She would have been wiser had she shown it to Edward, as she did the other. But she was ashamed to.

Another week brought her another letter.

"Private and Particular.

"PAINTED POST, June 13.

"MY DEAR CHILD,—I am *shocked* with the *levity* of your note, *without date*, which lies before me.

"Dear Psyche, fools make a *mock* of sin. How can you exult in your own *shame?* How can you live as the wife of a *man* of whom you know *nothing*, whose whole life is *suspicious* and a *scandal*, who is himself so *ashamed* of it that he does not admit *his own wife* to a knowledge of its *secret ways?* I cannot see how a child of *Christian parents* should be *so blinded* and *misled*.

"Rouse yourself in your strength, dear child. Ask your husband *honestly* and *bravely* what it is that he does in his *nightly orgies.* Do not think that we observed nothing in our *visit.* Do not think that we were *lulled* or put to *sleep* in our watch over our *sister. Never,* dear Psyche. We love you as much as ever. And we are *determined* to tear every shred of *mystery* from your life, once so *artless* and *pure.*

"Truly, your sister-mother,
"PRISCILLA."

"Sister-mother indeed!" said Psyche; and she wrote this letter:—

"DEAR PRIS,—If you will mind your business, I will mind mine.   P."

And she threw Priscilla's letter into the sea at high tide, torn into little bits. This was her second mistake.

This time this answer came:—

"PAINTED POST, June 21.

"MY DEAR LOST LAMB,—I have *spent* the *night* in *prayer* for you. This morning Agnes and Polly and I showed your *profligate letter* to our dear father. He has charged me to *write* what I *think* best to you.

"Is it not my *business* to care for the *life and soul* of a dear sister who has no *mother's love?* Am I not right when I fall on my *knees* to pray for her *welfare?* How could I *enjoy* the good of this life or the hopes of *another,* knowing that my sister is *eating* the *bread of wickedness* and drinking from the *cup of sin?* Shall the watchman desert his post because the *soldier sleeps?*

"*Ask yourself* why no person except the hireling tradesman ever *visits* at this *house* of luxury and *extravagance,* which your husband makes the prison-house of *your soul.*

"Ask yourself what is the fountain of this gold which he spends so shamelessly.

"Ask yourself, dear Psyche, what you would have said *two years ago* had any one told you that *you* should become the wife of a *counterfeiter* or a *forger* or a *gambler* or a *keeper of a dance-house* or a *detective,* or any other of those horrid things which are done in *secret.* If any one had said to you that you should have *pleasure* in those that do them, what would you *have said?* O my *dear lost lamb,* how often has that *sweet* text (see Romans i. 32) come back to me since I came to see you, in the *faint hope* that I might rescue my *lamb* even as a brand from the *burning!* My dear Psyche, will you not *turn* before it is *too late? Why will you die?*

"Thus asks and *prays* your own
"PRISCILLA."

"My own cat and dog!" said little Psyche scornfully. But she did not put the letter into the fire, nor did she tear it to shreds to throw them into the sea. I am very sorry; but, even in her wonder, she kept the letter hid away.

"What in the world did they find out about Edward that I do not know?" This was the first fatal question which Psyche asked herself.

"Forger, counterfeiter, detective, gambler—what do the vile creatures mean? They shall not say such horrid things about the best of men!"

"Ask yourself what is the fountain of this gold." Psyche had asked herself very often, and she did not know, and she knew she did not know. Edward was not lavish, and he was not parsimonious. She and he went over the bills together once a month, and when they were too large, they both took care that that should not happen again. And he gave her nice crisp bills to pay them with, and always gave her a separate sum for "P," which he said was her "private, personal, or peculiar share," which she had better not keep any account of. Where it all came from she did not know, and she knew she did not know; and she had promised not to ask him.

As for asking herself why nobody called to see her, she had asked that too, and she had no better answer. The minister did call once a year; but they had been out both times, and he had left his card. The doctor had called before Geoffrey was born, and after; but she had not asked him why nobody else called. She supposed it was the Boston way. Certainly she had called on nobody but on Mrs. Royall and Mrs. Flynn and a few more of her protegées. She was sure she did not want people to call on her, and she did not want to call on them.

Still the iron had entered her soul. And, as Satan ordered, for this week of all weeks, Edward was called away to New York; and although there were two letters a day from dear Edward, and very funny scraps from bills of fare and play-bills, and one or two new novels by post, and an English edition of the new "Morris," still her "earthly paradise" was a very gloomy paradise without him.

And every day the poor child read over Priscilla's venomous letter; and at last she went so far that she determined that she would ask him why nobody except the minister and the doctor ever came to see her.

Of course she did no such thing; for Friday night came, and—joy of joys!— Edward came. And Geoff was dragged out of his crib to see papa, and came down in his dear little flannel night-gown, and really knew papa, or was said to; and Geoff really grabbed at the new coral papa had brought to him, and held it in his hand and swayed it to and fro wildly, as a man very drunk would do; and they laughed happily over Geoff and put him to bed again; and then they sat and talked, and talked and sat, till long after any bedtime Psyche had ever dreamed of; and then they went to bed together, and as Psyche undressed, Edward read the story of the "Four Sons of Aymon" aloud to her. It was all as beautiful as it could be; and was she to bother him with talking about callers? Not she! She had him till Monday night, and she was not going to destroy her own paradise before then.

So there was one long, lovely Saturday, when he worked with her and she worked with him, and they went to the beach together, and went to drive together, and painted together, and in the evening they tried some new music that he had brought home; and he had a whole pile of lovely English and French letters which had come since he went away, and they had those to read together; and there was one German letter from his old Heidelberg friend, Welsted, and Psyche helped him puzzle out the words of the writing: he said she always guessed these riddles better than he did. And Welsted was married too, and he had a little girl baby, and made great fun about marrying her to Geoffrey. And they wrote an answer to Welsted, and it was midnight before they came round to the "Four Sons of Aymon" and to their bed.

And Sunday was another lovely day. They drove to church, and the drive was charming. They drove to Essex Woods, and that was charming. And Edward got out some of his old college diaries and read to her; and she fell to telling him about Ingham University. Oh dear! I do not know what they did not talk about. And it was midnight before they went to bed again.

Edward went right to sleep. Psyche had noticed that before. He would say, "God bless us, darling!" and he would be asleep in two seconds. But Psyche could not sleep. She had lost all her chances to ask him about the calls. She could not bear to wake him up and ask him. Nay, had she not promised him that she would not ask him? Not this very thing, perhaps, but what was just the same thing.

Why should she ask him? Why should she not find out without asking him? Priscilla seemed to know, but Priscilla had never asked him. How did Priscilla know? How did Priscilla know?—how? how? how? The poor child said this over to herself in words,—"How? how? how?"—and she fell asleep.

But she did not sleep well. All of a sudden, in a horrid dream, in which they were dragging Edward off to prison, she woke up. Oh, how glad she was to be awake! What in the world were they taking him to prison for? What had he done? Priscilla knew. Did Priscilla know? Why should not Psyche know?

Poor little Psyche! It was very still, and Edward was dead asleep. And one word from him would make her perfectly happy. And yet she did not dare ask him to speak that one word.

Why should she not be perfectly happy? Why should she disturb him at all? Why should she not keep her promise, and be perfectly happy too?

Dear little Psyche! Poor little Psyche! She got out of bed, and she stepped gently across the room to Edward's dressing-room, and she pushed the door to. It was the first time in her life that Psyche had ever tried to part herself from her husband. And she knew it was. And a cold shudder ran through her as she thought of this. But she was not born to be frightened by cold shudders. There was too much Lady Macbeth in her for that. She struck a match, lighted a candle, and sat for a minute thinking. Then she bravely took her husband's coat and drew from the breast-pocket that Russia leather letter-book which she gave him at Christmas. How little she thought then that she should be handling it stealthily at the dead of night!

She opened the book, which was full of letters. She seized the first:—

"MR. EDWARD ROSS, No. 999 State Street, Boston."

Then that was his office. She could drive down State Street some day and just look at the number. She set the candle on her knee to free her hand while she opened the letter.

"DEAR ROSS,—Could you spare me Orton for half an hour?

"E. J. F."

Miserable girl! She had violated all confidence—to learn nothing!

But Lady Macbeth went on.

"Mr. Edward Ross, 999 State Street:

"DEAR ROSS,—If you can come to club again, you will come to-day. Hedge reads, and Emerson and James will be there. We have not seen you for a year."

And she knew why he had not dined at club for a year, why he had spent every moment that he could spend at home. Miserable girl! It was for this that she had stolen out of bed!

So Lady Macbeth read No. 3.

"Mr. Edward Ross, 999 State Street:

"DEAR SIR,—We cannot match the turquoise here. But on the catalogue of Messrs. Roothan, Amsterdam, there are four such stones. Shall we telegraph them? We have very little time before July 31."

July 31 was her birthday. It was for this that she was reading her husband's secrets. Wretched Psyche!

Lady Macbeth went on.

"Private and Confidential.

"Edward Ross, Esq., 999 State Street:

Lady Macbeth paused, but her hand was in.

"DEAR SIR,—The committee met and read your letter with great care. Mr. Potter said that he had seen you on Tuesday, and that you expressed the same view then. I also laid before the committee General G——'s letter to you, and the telegram you had received from Syracuse. If you can persuade your friends to—"

Here the page ended, and Psyche had to turn over. As she turned, the candlestick tipped on her knee, fell bottom up upon the ground, and Psyche was in darkness.

What a noise it made! And what a guilty fool Psyche felt like! No Lady Macbeth now! But she folded the letter and put it back in the letter-case. She put the letter-case in the pocket, and folded the coat. She picked up the candle, and put it on the table. Then she slunk back into her bedroom. All this time Edward was crying out, "Dear Psyche, are you ill? What is it, dear?" He was out of bed, and was fumbling in the dark in Psyche's dressing-room. But the ways of the sea-shore home were not familiar to him.

When Psyche dared—that is, when she was at the foot of the bed—she cried out to Edward that nothing was wrong. She had had a bad dream, and was frightened, and had got up to strike a light, but she had not meant to call him. And he found her shivering on the bedside; and he cooed to her and comforted her, and made her promise to call him another time. And Psyche had just force enough to say sadly, "Call you—yes, if you are here." And then he sang to her a little crooning song his mother sang to him when he was a child, and poor Psyche cried herself to sleep.

CHAPTER V.

The next morning Psyche slept too heavily. She did not wake till Edward was out of bed. Then she started like a guilty thing. But she did not dare go into his dressing-room.

And he brought in the "Four Sons of Aymon," and read to her. Oh, she was as long as ever she could be about her dressing; but, alas! the breakfast-bell rang, and Edward ran into his room.

One minute,—it seemed forever,—then he came in with his coat, and with a look which tried to be comical, but was, oh, so sad! he pointed at the long swirl of spermaceti which ran from one end of it to the other.

Then he bent over the poor crying girl and kissed her, and kissed her again.

"How can you, Edward? I am so wicked—and such a fool!"

"Darling, you are not wicked at all, and it is I who am the fool."

"Dear Edward, hear me. I was perfectly happy till they came—"

"Sweetheart, you need not say so."

"Edward, hear me; read what they write to me. Read this. Read where they say you are a forger and a counterfeiter, a detective and a gambler."

"Really," said Edward, as he read, "they compliment me. The New York 'Observer' could not treat a man worse."

Psyche was amazed, and she saw that Edward was more amused than angry.

"Dear Edward, I am a fool. But I could not bear that Bloody Mary should know more of my own boy than I did."

"No, my darling," said he stoutly; "and there is no reason why you should. But hear that bell! Ellen is crazy that we shall come to breakfast. Finish your hair. I will find another coat; and at breakfast, as Miss Braddon says, I will tell you *all*."

And at breakfast he told her all. It was so little to tell that I am ashamed to have wasted ten thousand words without relieving the reader's anxiety.

As soon as Ellen had attended to the table and left the room, Edward said, "Dearest, all is that I am a greater fool than Clarence Hervey himself. I am the leading editor of the 'Daily Argus.' That is all."

Psyche fairly laid down her fork. "What a fool I am! I have read things I told you myself in the paper, yet I never dreamed that you put them there. But why keep such a secret from your poor little butterfly?"

"Why, my darling," said he more seriously,—"why, but that I wanted to have my butterfly to myself? You will see, dearest. God grant it may not be as I fear. But if—I am afraid—if one person knows where you live, he will know where I live. If one person knows, two will know. If two know, two hundred thousand will know. If they know, there is an end to breakfasts without door-bells, an end to German together, an end to water-colors and to music, an end to the pony-wagon and the drives. That was my only reason for trying to protect you from the necessity of keeping a secret. I thought, in that new part of Boston, if we called on nobody, nobody would call on us. So far I was not wrong. Then I took care at the office to have it understood that no messenger was to be sent to my house. I bit off old Folger's head one day when he offered to send me a proof-sheet. Then I thought if we sent out 'No cards,' if I could only make you happy without 'receiving,' my friends would not know where to find me, and so my enemies would never know, nor the intermediate mass who are neither friends nor enemies. A little skill in May was enough to keep my name out of the Directory, excepting with the office address. Indeed, I thought if I did my six hours' work there between nine and three every night, it was all the world had a right to ask of me. But all this has made you wretched, so it has been all wrong, and it shall come to an end. You shall have a state dinner-party next Saturday."

Psyche cried and cried and cried, as if her heart would break. And Edward cried a little too.

"But why not go on so now?" said she. "I can keep a secret." This she said proudly, though she blushed as she said it. "Wild horses shall not draw it from me."

"No," said Edward sadly, "I know wild horses will not drag it from my darling; but I know they will try, and I do not choose to have her torn by wild horses: she has suffered enough from the pulling and hauling of three wild asses."

And so it was all settled that they should begin to see people. All was as clear as light between them now, and the new dynasty began.

And for a month or two there was no great change. At first it was only that Ross brought out one or two gentlemen with him to spend Sunday. They made the house very pleasant, and dear little Psyche did the honors beautifully. Then they whispered round what a charming home it was. And the Beverly people, some of whom are very nice persons, found out what a pretty neighbor they had, and that it was Ross of the "Argus," and they called, and asked to tea, and then Psyche and Edward returned the calls, and asked to tea.

It was not till they went back to Roxbury that the real change came. Then was it that before breakfast the door-bell began to ring; and women with causes, and men out of employment, and inventors with inventions, began to wait in the ante-room till Mr. E. Ross came downstairs. Then was it that he poured down his hasty cup of coffee, and ran to be rid of them. Then was it that councilmen came out as soon as breakfast was over to arrange private schemes for thwarting the aldermen; and that while the councilmen arranged, aldermen called and waited for Mr. E. Ross to be at leisure, because they wanted to make plans for thwarting the council. Then was it that, from morning to night, candidates for the House and candidates for the Senate came for private conferences, and had to be let out from different doors lest they should meet each other. Then was it that men who had letters of introduction from Japan and Formosa and Siberia and Aboukuta sat in Psyche's parlor six or seven hours at a time, illustrating the customs of those countries, and what Mr. Lowell calls "a certain air of condescension observable in foreigners." Then was it that Psyche received calls from wives of senators and daughters of congressmen, to say in asides to her that if Mr. E. Ross could find it in his way to say this, he would so much oblige thus and so. Then was it that, trying to screen him from bores, she received all the women who sold Lives of Christ, and all the agents who exhibited copies of maps or heliotypes. Then was it that, when the ponies came to the door, railroad presidents drew up, who just wanted a minute to talk about their new bonds. Then was it that, after the ponies had been sent back to the stable, grand ladies drew up to send in cards to Psyche, and to persuade her to take tables at fairs and to be vice-president of almshouses. Then was it that every Saturday Psyche gave a charming literary dinner, not bad in its way; and the counterpart of this was that Psyche and Edward dined at other people's houses four days out of the remaining six. The sixth day Edward was kept down town for some of the engagements these wretches had forced him into. Thus was it in the end that moths ate up the camel's-hair pencils, and no one ever found it out; that the upper G string in the piano rusted off, and no one discovered it; that Bridget Flynn put ten volumes of Grillparzer into the furnace-fire, and nobody missed them; and that all the ferns in the fern-house died, and nobody wept for them.

From early morning round to early morning Psyche never saw her lover-husband, except as he and she gorged a hurried and broken breakfast, or as he took in to dinner some lady he did not care for, and as she, at her end of the table, talked French or Cochin Chinese to some man who had brought letters of introduction.

She knew what her husband's business was and who his friends were. But, for all intents and purposes, she had lost him forever.

As for the three step-sisters at Painted Post, they went to a Sunday-School picnic one day, and fell off a precipice and were killed.